"DON'T YOU BELIEVE IN LOVE?" HE ASKED

"Oh, yes," Philippa answered. "That's why I . . . I don't want to anticipate marriage. I suppose you think that's stupid of me?"

"Extremely stupid in this day and age. But it's a stupidity I'm glad for." His arms came around her again, cradling her tenderly. "Darling," he said huskily.

She returned his kisses until every throbbing nerve of her body begged to be mastered. But he seemed to remember her earlier assertion and slowly broke their embrace.

"You'd better take me home, Mr. Lyons," Philippa said shakily.

"Don't you think you could call me Marius?"

"I've never thought of you that way."

"At least you have thought of me?" he said, his hand warm and intimate on hers.

"With quite a lot of dislike!"

He laughed heartily. "You're not frightened of me, are you, Philippa? It's one of the things . . . the many things I like about you."

HARLEQUIN
PREMIERE AUTHOR EDITIONS

These books may be available at your local bookseller.

For a free catalog listing all titles currently available,
send your name and address to:

Harlequin Reader Service
P.O. Box 52040, Phoenix, AZ 85072-9988
Canadian address: Stratford, Ontario N5A 6W2

ROBERTA LEIGH

HEART
OF THE LION

Harlequin Books

TORONTO • NEW YORK • LONDON
AMSTERDAM • PARIS • SYDNEY • HAMBURG
STOCKHOLM • ATHENS • TOKYO • MILAN

First Harlequin edition published January 1975

ISBN 0-373-80653-1

This HARLEQUIN PREMIERE AUTHOR
EDITION published September 1983

Original hardcover edition published in 1974
by Mills & Boon Limited.

CHAPTER ONE

The vast glass and steel skyscraper of Lyon Publications dominated one entire intersection at the end of Fleet Street, in the same way that its newspapers and magazines dominated the market.

As always when she emerged from the Underground station each morning and had her first glimpse of it, Philippa Rogers found it hard to believe her good luck that she should be working there. And not as a cub reporter either, but as assistant to Mrs. Jessica Hibberd, doyen of all the columnists referred to as "sob sisters".

Philippa had been dismayed when she had first been assigned to the page. Not for her to deal with the lovelorn letters and plaintive cries of heartbroken females clamouring for advice. She had come to Fleet Street to report the news and nothing less would satisfy her. However, the Features Editor had seen things differently.

"Wait till you start working for Jessie before you decide you don't want the job," he had informed her. "You'll learn more from her about being a reporter than you will writing up petty crime or going out with the Fire Brigade!"

"There are other stories than petty crime and fires," she had protested.

"Not for you, young lady. Those are the stories all junior reporters cut their teeth on for at least a year! You can count yourself lucky Mrs. Hibberd saw that piece you wrote on old-age pensioners. She liked your style and asked if you could be assigned to her."

"Don't I have any say in the matter?"

"Of course you do," Kennedy Jones had smiled. "You can hand in your notice."

"Oh no, I don't want to do that."

"Then be a good girl and do as I say." The man's smile was

genuine now. "It never entered my head you'd turn it down. It's a feather in your cap to be chosen."

"I don't see why. Working on an advice column isn't going to teach me anything about reporting."

"It will teach you how to understand people and situations – and that's what being a reporter is all about. Not just reporting the news, but doing it in such a way that people can understand and feel it."

"The facts should speak for themselves," she had replied firmly. "The bias of a writer should never be apparent."

"Now you're talking like a cheap course on journalism! Marius Lyon *wants* his writers to be biased – providing the bias follows his direction, of course! Every one of his publications has its own personality and its own prejudices. There isn't a paper or magazine in the world today that gives you plain, un-biased reporting."

It was a truth with which Philippa was forced to agree, albeit reluctantly, for she mourned the passing of the truly impartial newspaper. Still, once she had made a name for herself, she intended to be known for her factual reporting. But until she was established enough to give orders instead of take them, she would have to do as she was told.

"Well," Kennedy Jones had interrupted her reverie, "will you work as Mrs. Hibberd's assistant, or do I offer the job to someone else?"

"I'll take it," she said, and presented herself in Mrs. Hibberd's office the same morning.

Jessica Hibberd, or "Dear Jessie" as she was known to some five million readers, was so much like everyone's idea of a country aunt as to be almost a parody of it. She was a plump woman in her late fifties, with softly waving grey hair above a lined, unpowdered face. Her well-corseted figure seemed made for its uniform of heather-tweed suit and sensible brogues, and was as much a part of her appearance as her white shirt blouse, caught at the throat by a cameo brooch. But her unsophisticated appearance hid a mind whose sharpness was felt by anyone who did not follow her orders, for in everything connected with

6

her column she demanded total obedience.

Mrs. Hibberd's dedication to her readers was as committed as theirs to her, and within a few weeks of working for her, Philippa understood why. No cry for help was ever considered too weak to be ignored, and whether it came from an eighty-year-old man living in a hamlet in Cornwall, or the wife of a politician privately inquiring what she should wear on a forth-coming trip with her husband to South America, it received the same serious attention and considered answer. Too much so, Philippa sometimes thought, for many of the requests which the "Dear Jessie" column received could easily have been dealt with by other sections of the newspaper.

"You let people take advantage of you," Philippa had remonstrated on one occasion.

"I'm here to help."

"That doesn't mean doing someone else's job. We've dealt with three letters about food prices that should never have come to us at all. You should have sent them straight back to the editorial page."

"I think we ought to know about food prices," Jessica Hibberd had said calmly. "Everything that affects our lives – whether it's the cost of bread or a new height for sink units – can add to one's stress, and we're here to deal with stress – whether it comes from inflation, abortion or a washing machine that won't work!"

"I still think you let everyone impose on you," Philippa had grumbled. "You do far too much."

"Then you'll have to help me," came the casual answer. "You're more than capable of dealing with some of the letters on your own."

To be allowed to reply to any "Dear Jessie" letters without having to get them vetted by Jessica Hibberd first, was a rare honour indeed, and one given to only two other girls out of the staff of twelve. Remembering the reluctance with which she had come to work on this page, Philippa marvelled that her attitude should have changed so much in such a short space of time. She understood now what Kennedy Jones had meant

7

when he had said that learning about people's problems would help her to be a better reporter. He could just as well have said that compassion would help her to be a better person, for anything that increased one's awareness of others must inevitably be reflected in the quality of one's work.

Six months after joining the Aunt Jessie page, Philippa was given the chance of returning to the News Desk, but by then she was so involved with what she was doing that she turned it down. Jessica Hibberd made no comment on the decision, but a week later, Philippa found herself being given the chance of writing the lead reply in the column.

From then on she was regarded as Mrs. Hibberd's personal assistant, and was jokingly referred to by the other girls as "Jessie Junior". She took the teasing in her stride, and the diligent research which many letters demanded was more than compensated for by the occasional letter of thanks which she received. Sometimes the writer expressed the hope of meeting "Dear Jessie" face to face, but this was something Mrs. Hibberd refused to countenance, and warned Philippa against ever doing so.

"You can only give your best advice if you remain uninvolved and unbiased," she had said, "and lack of bias is our strongest asset."

"It also makes us the only unbiased page Mr. Lyon publishes!" Philippa had retorted, a remark which made the older woman laugh.

"Mr. Lyon's background doesn't encourage him to be impartial. Any man who has worked his way up from nothing must have enormous belief in himself and what he's doing. And that kind of belief doesn't go with an unbiased attitude."

Philippa was remembering this remark as she walked through the marble entrance hall of Lyon Publications, and went up in one of the lifts to the twelfth floor. It was strange to think she had worked here for a year yet had never met the man who controlled this vast empire. In fact, now she came to think of it, Jessica Hibberd was one of the few people she knew who had ever seen Marius Lyon. But then most newspaper tycoons fought shy of personal appearances. They had no compunction in splashing everyone else's name and photograph across the pages of their papers and magazines, but they used their own position to make sure the same thing did not happen to them.

She walked into her office and hung up her coat in the cupboard, then without bothering to look at herself in the mirror on the inside of its door, sat down at her typewriter. Thank goodness Mrs. Hibberd had managed to stop her own suite of offices from being turned into open-plan accommodation and it spoke for the regard in which she was held that her request had been granted without argument.

"I refuse to work in an open field," she had protested. "I've got used to my rabbit warren and I don't intend to have it changed."

It had, Philippa knew, resulted in a somewhat stormy meeting with Marius Lyon himself, and he had – to everyone's surprise – given in.

"A pity more people don't stand up to him," Mrs. Hibberd had commented when she had returned to the office. "It might stop him from being quite such a dictator."

"Lyon by temperament as well as name!" Philippa grinned.

"He looks like one, too."

"Does he?" Philippa had asked curiously, but had received no further information, for a telephone call interrupted their conversation, and when it was resumed, it had been about the column.

For some reason Philippa was thinking of her unseen and unknown employer as she began to open the letters piled on her desk. Three hundred and ten of them altogether, and this was only the first post. She swung round and peered through the glass partition: her counterpart in the next office had a similar pile. If the letters continued to arrive at this rate they would need to increase their staff. She frowned, wondering whether there would come a time when the Accounts Department would veto a further increase in staff. Since she had been here they had already taken on two extra secretaries, and short of standardising far more letters than they were now doing, they would shortly

9

have to take on another one.

She glanced at her wristwatch, the frown changing to surprise as she saw it was ten-thirty. It was unlike Mrs. Hibberd to be late. If anything, she had a tendency to arrive at the office before anyone else, and staying later too. Not that she had done this in the last few weeks. Now she thought about it, Philippa remembered that Jessica Hibberd had frequently gone home earlier than anyone else.

She was sipping a mid-morning cup of coffee before the columnist finally appeared. On the surface she looked her usual imperturbable self, but as she came to stand by Philippa's desk to look through some of the answers that had been roughly pencilled out and attached to each letter, Philippa saw that the plump hands were trembling.

"Is anything wrong?" she asked.

"No, dear." Jessica Hibberd's voice was as calm as ever, and without saying anything further she bustled into her own office. For the rest of the day she worked with ferocious energy, and by five o'clock everyone around her was exhausted, though she herself showed no sign of fatigue as she called Philippa into her office to discuss the letters to be published in Wednesday's edition of the paper.

"These are *my* suggestions," Philippa said, and handed some typewritten sheets across the desk. "I had to condense the lead letter quite a bit, but the rest are virtually untouched."

Jessica Hibberd glanced at them quickly, and Philippa noticed that the brown eyes kept moving to the telephone, as though expecting it to ring.

"I like all your choice of letters except the lead one," the woman said. "We can do with a stronger opening. I'm dealing with a letter just now which might be worth printing. It's from a man whose wife has left him, and he finds it impossible to live alone."

"I didn't think that was a problem that affected men!"

"More men than women commit suicide out of loneliness," Jessica Hibberd replied. "Women are much stronger creatures – I suppose they've had to be."

"Have you written the reply to the letter yet?" Philippa asked.

"No. I'll do it now. But I wanted to make sure you agree with my choice."

"I wouldn't dare not to," Philippa smiled.

The telephone rang and Jessica Hibberd snatched it up as though it were about to explode. The colour seeped from her skin as she listened, and without a word Philippa went to the cupboard which stood beneath the window and took out a bottle of whisky. She poured some into a glass and placed it into Jessica Hibberd's hand.

"Drink it," she mouthed, and bent forward as though ready to see that her words were carried out.

The glass was raised to pallid lips and at the same time Mrs. Hibberd replaced the receiver.

"If that was an obscene call . . ." Philippa began.

"It was the hospital." Jessica Hibberd's voice was faint but firm. "My husband was admitted this morning and they just telephoned to say they will be operating on him in the morning."

Philippa could not hide her astonishment. "I never knew Mr. Hibberd was ill."

"It isn't something we talk about."

"I'm sorry, I didn't mean to pry."

"Don't be silly. You're the last person in the world to pry." The grey head lowered over the desk so that the eyes were hidden. "He has a heart condition. For a long time we've been debating whether or not he should have an operation – there's a lot of risk involved and we weren't sure. But now there's no choice. It has to be done."

"Would you like me to come with you to the hospital?"

The grey head lifted. "That's very kind of you, but I'd prefer you to stay here if you will and write the column for me."

"*All* of it?"

"You can do it, Philippa. It's what I've been training you for."

Philippa was speechless. She had often wondered how she would feel if she were asked to do the whole column, but even thinking of it had given her butterflies in the stomach. Yet now that anticipation had become reality, she felt no fear. Perhaps it was because the chance had stemmed from Mrs. Hibberd's personal misfortune.

"I'll be glad to do it for you," she said. "Do you have any notes you'd like me to follow?"

"None. I want the page to be entirely your own. Just remember what I said to you before about men sometimes being more affected by loneliness than women."

Promising not to forget, Philippa followed the old woman down the corridor, though in reality she was more concerned over Mrs. Hibberd's problem. She remembered the few remarks that had been bandied around the office about her employer's private life. No children, a flat in town and a house in the country, both shared by a husband some ten years her senior who worked at some unspecified job in the city.

"Has Mr. Hibberd been ill long?" she asked as they waited for the lift to appear.

"He's always had a heart condition, but it's become progressively worse in the last few years."

"It must be an awful decision to make – whether to live as an invalid or take a chance and have an operation."

"Frank would have had the operation years ago if the choice had been left to him," Jessica Hibberd said tremulously. "But he knew I was frightened for him, that I'd rather have him an invalid alive than . . ."

The lift doors opened and she stepped inside.

"Are you sure you'll be all right on your own?" Philippa asked anxiously. "I can come with you to the hospital and do the column later tonight."

"I'd rather be on my own, thank you."

"At least give me the name of the hospital. Then I can phone and – "

"The National Heart Hospital," came the reply as the lift doors closed and put an end to further conversation.

Trying to dismiss her anxiety, Philippa returned to the office and the writing of the column. It was more difficult than she had expected, partly because she felt no sympathy with the writer of the letter which she had been instructed to make the leading one. The tone of it struck her as whining, and she wondered if Jessica Hibberd would have chosen it had she been in her normal state of mind. The urge to put another letter in its place was strongly tempting, and she picked out several that she liked before deciding that to do so might be construed as arrogance.

No, come what may she had to work out a decent reply to the letter she had been given. Once again she put fresh paper in the typewriter and set to work.

Never had words been so difficult to find, and the typewriter keys only clacked spasmodically for the next hour. Eventually perseverance won the day, and with satisfaction she surveyed the foolscap page that contained the carefully edited letter and her reply to it. Clipping the sheet to the rest of the column, she rang for one of the messenger boys to take it down to be typeset. Because of the great importance attached to the "Dear Jessie" page, no sub-editing of it was allowed, and any alterations that had to be done – due to space and any layout requirements – were always dealt with by Mrs. Hibberd herself. Having seen some of her own copy badly mangled when she had been on the Features page, Philippa enjoyed knowing that what she had written tonight would not be ruthlessly slashed.

Putting the cover over her typewriter she crossed to the mirror that hung rakishly on the wall and ran a comb through her thick, beech-brown hair. Even in the dingy glass its rich lustre could not be denied, and it rippled to her shoulders like a heavy fall of satin; but it was the unexpected streak of silver that sprang up from her forehead which attracted one's attention, for it looked as though a beam of light had been trapped among the chestnut strands. Ever since she could remember she had had this silver streak, and though it had caused her some teasing as a child, she had now come to accept it and even to like the distinction it gave her. She had the colouring and features associated with a true brunette; creamy skin and large sherry-coloured eyes that glowed gold when she was happy, and darker brown when she was not; a faintly tip-tilted nose and a large, well-shaped mouth that added piquancy to her expression. She was slightly taller than average, being five feet seven without her shoes, but she refused to make any concession to her height, and when fashion decreed high heels she wore them, knowing how well they emphasised her shapely legs.

During her time in the Features section she had had to walk daily through male dominated offices, where she had run the gamut of some hundred pairs of inquisitive eyes and, after an initial embarrassment, had learned to accept the fact that firm, full breasts above a tiny waist – allied to a swinging walk – attracted wolf-whistles and pleasurable comment.

Because she had been the only girl in a family of three brothers, Philippa had never been embarrassed by the physical, and had accepted her voluptuous body with the same easy casualness that she had accepted her brothers' strong, tanned physique and fearless attitude to life. The fact that two of them had settled as farmers in Africa, and the third to the rigours of being an oilman in Alaska, was the only sadness in a life that had so far been remarkably contented. Too much so, she sometimes thought, and wondered if an unrequited love affair would give more warmth to her writing. Working on the "Dear Jessie" page was the next best thing, for at least one suffered vicariously.

She swung away from the mirror and went to pick up her handbag, stopping as one of the messenger boys came in.

"Mrs. Hibberd around?" he asked.

"She left ages ago."

"That's torn it. There's a girl who wants to see her. A damsel in distress," he grinned.

"Mrs. Hibberd never sees anyone like that. That's one of the rules."

"Rules are meant to be broken." The cheeky reply was offset by another grin.

"Well, I'm afraid she isn't here, so you'd better tell the caller that she's wasting her time."

The boy went out of the office and then almost immediately put his head around the door again. "You'll be able to tell her yourself," he muttered, and disappeared at a run as a slim, dark-haired girl with a tragic look on her face dashed precipitately into the room.

"Mrs. Hibberd, thank heavens I've found you. If *you* can't help me, I'll kill myself!"

CHAPTER TWO

Philippa stared at the intruder in dismay, her hope of being able to get rid of the girl dissolving as she recognised the signs of hysteria in the pale face and trembling body.

"I'm afraid I can't help you," she said quickly. "I'm not – "

"I know you don't normally see people, but I'm desperate. You've *got* to help me."

"Have you written to us?" Philippa asked, disconcerted by the pleading on the unformed face in front of her. The girl could not be more than eighteen, and had the fragile dewy look of an unplucked flower. It was a fanciful simile and she dismissed it with a shrug and hardened her heart to the tearful pleading in the soft voice.

"I can't give advice off the cuff," she said firmly. "We never do. Never. You must write to us. We reply to every letter we receive and – "

"I haven't time to wait for a reply. I've got to have my answer now – tonight, otherwise it will be too late."

"Why didn't you write to us before?"

"I couldn't. The problem didn't arise until a little while ago – three hours to be exact." The girl flung out her hand and caught Philippa's in a tight grasp. "You can't refuse to help me. That's what you're here for, isn't it?"

"I'm not refusing. I'm merely telling you that we only deal with problems by letter."

"You can't make such ridiculous rules when you're dealing with people," the girl retorted. "Human beings can't be filed away in folders!"

"They can, you know," Philippa tried to keep her voice humorous. "Why don't you go home and write to us? You can do it downstairs if you like and leave the letter at the desk. We'll deal with it first thing in the morning."

"It'll be too late by then," the girl cried. "I'll either be married or buried!"

The incongruity of the words was offset by the dramatic way they were said, and realising the girl was hysterical, Philippa tried to pacify her. "I'm sure things can't be as bad as all that," she said gently, and waited for the floodgates to open.

They did. Wide. Unleashing a torrent of emotion that went ill with the prosaic office with its mundane furniture and battered typewriters. Philippa had encountered similar stories many times before: an eighteen-year-old loving unsuitably and a parent disapproving and being strong enough to give that disapproval force. But with Cathy Joyce – as the girl called herself – the story was slightly different, for the parents were replaced by an uncle with whom she lived and of whom she seemed to be terribly afraid. Her mother had died when she was twelve and her father had married a much younger woman who, not wanting to be saddled with a child, had eventually succeeded in persuading the uncle to offer them the use of his own home.

"He's worse than any father could be," the girl cried. "He lives in the Middle Ages and he regards anyone under twenty-five as still being in the schoolroom!"

"I'm sure you're exaggerating."

"I'm not! He treats me like a baby, and Celia encourages him."

"Celia?" Philippa queried.

"My stepmother. I thought she'd be glad to get rid of me, but now I know why she isn't. If I were married she wouldn't be able to go on living with my uncle. She'd be forced to move out and make a life of her own. That's why she wants to keep me a baby. And I'm not a baby, Mrs. Hibberd, I'm eighteen and I know my own mind."

"I'm not – "

"Don't say you won't help me. You've got to tell me what to do." Cathy Joyce stared beseechingly into Philippa's face. "I love Alan so much. If I can't marry him I'll kill myself!"

Philippa sighed and went to sit at her desk. With a barrier of teak between them she looked at her young visitor more closely, hoping to find in her appearance some clue as to her background. But the casual mode of present-day fashion made this difficult. The long dark hair and unmade-up face, the plain white mackintosh and dark sweater beneath it, was a uniform one encountered any time of the day in almost any place. The voice was educated though, with a breathy ingenuousness so often found in boarding-school types. No State-school product here.

"Where do you live?" she asked gently.

"In London. What's that got to do with it?"

"I'm trying to find out your background. It's important to know that before giving any advice."

"I've told you my background. I live with my stepmother and my uncle. *She* wants to keep me a child, and *he* wants me to go to university and develop my mind."

"Do they know you're in love?"

"Of course they do! I've known Alan for a year, and since I've met him I haven't looked at anyone else."

"Are you sure *he* loves *you*?"

"He wants to marry me. It was his idea we elope. That's why I'm here. Because I don't know whether I should."

Here at last was the all-important reason, and faced with it, Philippa played for time. Only rarely did Jessica Hibberd give an unequivocal yes or no to any question put to her. "You need to be a very special person in order to accept a cut-and-dried answer," she frequently said, "and someone who is capable of accepting and acting on your advice isn't the type who needs to ask for it! That's why it's always best to give alternatives. To say 'Yes, if . . .' or 'no, but . . .' Then you're leaving people with an option."

It was advice with which Philippa had not always agreed, privately feeling that very often people would welcome being firmly told what to do, as she would firmly like to tell this girl in front of her. Yet to say she should elope could be dangerous – as dangerous as telling her to remain where she was. Philippa frowned. What was it the girl had said about being married or buried by the morning?

"What does your boy-friend do?" she asked, playing for time.

"He's a mechanic. He works in a garage in North London. He's in charge of the maintenance and repair department. He's brilliant with cars."

"Then he's earning enough to keep you?"

"Money's no problem," the girl replied with a toss of her head. "It's only my uncle who makes such a fuss about it."

"Why exactly does he object to Alan?"

"I told you. Because he wants me to go to university."

"That's not such a bad idea."

"I'm not interested in getting a degree. I want to get married and take care of Alan. I love him and I want to live with him. If I can't do that I might as well be dead!" She burst into noisy sobs and Philippa jumped up and came round the side of the desk.

"Crying won't help you to solve your problem, Cathy. And I certainly can't talk to you while you're making so much noise. Wait here a minute and I'll get some coffee."

She ran out of the office and down the corridor to a group of vending machines set in an alcove, returning with two cups of coffee and a packet of biscuits.

Cathy had stopped crying and had made some attempt to repair the ravages caused by her tears. She looked more than ever like an unhappy puppy, an effect heightened by the soft dark hair which fell like spaniel's ears either side of her face, and the long-lashed brown eyes, still awash with tears.

"Drink the coffee and tell me the whole story again," Philippa said. "But cut out the drama and stick to facts."

The girl seemed about to protest, but something on Philippa's face decided her against it, and she sipped her coffee and made an effort to collect her thoughts before doing as she was told. Repeated more calmly, the story remained predominantly the same: an unhappy eighteen-year-old dominated by a stepmother who didn't love her and an uncle who persisted in seeing her as he wanted her to be rather than as she really was. Ambitious and intent on making money, he believed everyone should stretch themselves to the fullest, both mentally and physically, and for this reason was insisting his niece accept the university place she had been offered, despite the fact that she had no academic aspirations.

Alan had come into Cathy's life a year ago. From that time on they had been inseparable, and though Philippa gathered that the girl had made no secret of her friendship with him, she was pretty sure she had not disclosed the frequency with which she was seeing him, nor the strength of her attachment. Because of this, her announcement that she wanted to marry him had come as an unwelcome surprise. When pleading and argument had failed to make Cathy promise to stop seeing him, her uncle had resorted to firmer tactics, and had forbidden Alan the house, while keeping Cathy locked up in it.

Try as she would, Philippa could see no reason for such behaviour. Not only was Cathy of age and able to please herself whom she married, but the unknown Alan seemed a steady young man, able to maintain a wife. Skilled motor mechanics were at a premium and he would never be hard-up for money or out of a job. It was ludicrous that all the people concerned in this unhappy saga could not sit down together and discuss the situation reasonably. She sighed. So many older people refused to realise that by putting their own ambitions on to young shoulders they were only doing them a disservice. Though she appreciated the value of higher education, she knew that not everyone wanted it, and the attitude of Cathy's uncle smacked of dictatorship rather than paternalistic interest.

"Why is it so important for you to make a decision tonight?" she asked the girl.

"Alan has given me an ultimatum. He says if I love him I'll run away with him."

"You could equally well tell him that if he loves you he'll wait for you."

"He's already waited a year."

"You're only eighteen," Philippa persisted. "It wouldn't be so terrible if he waited a bit longer."

"Age has nothing to do with it," the girl said angrily. "You're as bad as my stepmother."

"I'm merely suggesting that if you and Alan waited, your uncle and stepmother might change their minds – "

"They'll never change! I told you, Celia wants to keep me in the nursery for ever."

"If you listened to your uncle and went to university," Philippa insisted, "they'd soon realise you weren't a child. I'm sure that in a matter of six months you'd be able to get engaged to Alan with their blessing."

The girl's reply was short and rude, and Philippa reddened. "I'm sorry I'm not giving you the answer you want to hear."

"You're on their side, that's why!"

"I'm not on anybody's side. You told me the situation and I'm trying to make you see it isn't the end of the world if you don't elope with Alan tonight."

"It's the end of *my* world," the girl cried. "That's what you don't understand. Alan's been asking me to elope with him for six months, and now he's given me an ultimatum. If I won't do it, he'll stop seeing me."

"I'm sure he doesn't mean it," Philippa said soothingly. "Not if he loves you."

"He does mean it. He knows my uncle, and he says if I won't stand up to him now, I never will. That's why I've got to make up my mind."

Philippa stared at Cathy. "When people write to us for advice it's because they're faced with alternatives and don't know which one to take. But you don't have that sort of problem. Alan wants you to elope with him and you want to marry him. So why do you need me to tell you what to do? As you said yourself, you're old enough to vote and old enough to get married."

The girl jumped to her feet, her face alight with happiness. "You don't know what it means to me to hear you say that! You're the first person I've been able to talk to for months."

"Haven't you any friends?"

"No. They're all in – " The girl stopped abruptly and came across the room to Philippa's side. "That's why it was so important for me to see you. I read your column every week – it's the only reason I get the paper – and when this happened with

Alan I felt you were the one person who could help me."

"I haven't told you anything," Philippa cautioned. "I've just tried to make you see the situation the way it is."

"You've certainly done that. You've made everything clear. I don't know why I didn't see it for myself. I mean, Alan and I love each other and no one can stop us getting married. It isn't even as if I'm running away from my parents. It's only a stepmother and an uncle." She made for the door, paused on the threshold to give another beaming smile, and then disappeared from sight.

At a more leisurely pace Philippa followed her visitor down the corridor. It was unfortunate that tonight of all nights Jessica Hibberd had not been in the office. She frowned, wondering if the woman's advice to the girl would have differed from her own. It seemed a strange story for today, as though time had stood still in Cathy Joyce's household, but there had been the ring of conviction in what the girl had said, and Philippa was sure that though her story might have been exaggerated, it was basically truthful.

Why should the girl's uncle object so strongly to his niece getting married? Did he really think a university education superseded everything else? The stepmother's reasons for keeping Cathy at home were valid and need not be questioned, though they could certainly be discounted. That brought Philippa back to the uncle again, and the reason for his treating Cathy as a child, rather than as someone who knew her own mind. Perhaps the girl was ill; was this why he didn't want her to marry? Philippa's frown grew deeper and though she tried to dismiss her troubled thoughts, they remained with her, and she began to regret that she had not kept completely quiet and refused to give any opinion at all.

In an effort to quell her anxiety she scanned the pages of the telephone directory. If she could speak to Cathy she might be able to set her own mind at rest. But there were hundreds of Joyces in the telephone directory, and she soon recognised the hopelessness of her task. Besides, she did not even know the name of Cathy's uncle. Angry that she had not thought to take the girl's address, she again tried to push her out of her mind, and in an effort to do so, switched on the television. She would tell Mrs. Hibberd the whole story tomorrow. Not that it would make any difference by then, Philippa thought with sudden conviction, and had a premonition of Cathy Joyce driving beside her boy-friend Alan on their way to an unknown future, but a future in which they would be together.

CHAPTER THREE

Philippa's desire to tell Jessica Hibberd of her meeting with Cathy Joyce did not materialise. Arriving at the office in the morning she found a message on her desk asking he to deal with all office matters, and for the rest of the day she was kept too busy to think of anything except the column. But late in the afternoon she took a taxi to the National Heart Hospital and, in the waiting room on the first floor, soon found herself facing her employer.

"I know I should have telephoned you first instead of coming here," she apologised, "but I felt I had to see you personally and find out how your husband was."

"How kind you are. But there's no news yet. I'm afraid. I'm not sure whether that's good or bad."

"I'm sure it must be good." Philippa hesitated and then said awkwardly: "You've no need to worry about the column. Everything's fine."

"I don't care if it isn't! Nothing's important except Frank."

"I know how you feel." She saw Mrs. Hibberd glance at her watch as though impatient to return to the ward. "I'll phone you later tonight, if I may," she went on, "and if there's anything I can do . . ."

"Pray," Mrs. Hibberd said quietly. "That's all anyone can do now."

Soberly Philippa returned to the office, her mood of sadness only starting to lift as she set about preparations for the next column. Working for a newspaper was like having to feed a perpetually ravenous monster: as soon as one was over, another had to be made ready. She stared at the pile of letters on her desk. It was all very well to be a career woman, but sometimes one longed for the anonymity of one's home and the reassuring haven of one special pair of arms. Did men feel this way too?, she mused. Did they ever look up from their office work and wish they were in the comfort of their home or the peace of their garden?

Through the glass partition she saw Kennedy Jones stride by. Difficult to believe *he* could ever long for peace and quiet. All he cared about was the newspaper and the rising circulation that reflected its success. The door opened and he came in, a tall man in his late forties, with eyes that were perpetually red-rimmed with tiredness, and the odour of tobacco clinging to his suit.

"Still happy dispensing advice to the lovelorn?" he asked. "Or are you ready to join the land of the living?"

"If that's an offer to return to Features – "

"It is."

"Then the answer's still no! I'm enjoying myself too much here."

"You're crazy." He grinned, "Care to join me for a drink later on?"

"That's an offer I'll be delighted to accept. What time?"

"I'll buzz you when I'm free. I'm on my way to see Marius Lyon."

Sitting at a small table in a wine bar with Kennedy Jones later that evening, she knew something had happened to upset him since their earlier meeting.

"Had a rousting from Big Brother?" she asked, sipping a glass of sparkling Sancerre.

"I never even got to see him. One of his family's been injured in a car crash and he's at the hospital."

"I never knew he had any family."

"That's one of the compensations of being a newspaper tycoon. You wash other people's dirty linen in public, but you can keep your own out of it!"

"Tell me more," she asked, sensing a scandal. "Did his wife run off with the chauffeur?"

"He isn't married. It's his – " He stopped as a portly man came over to greet them.

It was Jack Lane, Features Editor of their strongest rival paper, and Philippa listened with amusement as the two men – who were well-known Fleet Street opponents and daily tried to out-scoop each other – exchanged ribald greetings.

"We had some interesting photographs of Lyon brought in to

us the other day," Jack said laconically, easing himself into a vacant chair beside Philippa. "Taken with a telephoto lens and showing him in a highly complicated position with the third Mrs. – " His voice dropped as he mentioned the wife of a Greek tycoon.

"Lyon's been in many complicated positions," Kennedy Jones replied, "but his best one is being at the top of Lyon Publications!"

"It's a *protected* position," the other man agreed, and gave such a heavy sigh that Philippa could not help chuckling. "What's amusing you, young lady?" he asked.

"You both are," she replied. "You know very well if you publish anything about Mr. Lyon we'd publish our own interesting photographs of *your* estimable boss!"

"What an unethical thing to do! It's dog eat dog in this game."

"Don't you mean dog not eating dog?"

It was his turn to chuckle. "One day I'll retire and spill the beans about everybody!"

"You'll have to leave the country if you do."

"If my tax bills go up any more I may be forced to do so." He rubbed the side of his nose and looked at Kennedy Jones. "I hear Lyon's out to get another Sunday newspaper. Is it true?"

"If it were I wouldn't tell you."

"You're too loyal to him," Jack grumbled.

"That's what he pays me for."

"Pays damn well too: I'll say that for him. Still, what else can he do with his millions? He's got no family to leave it to." He signalled for a further round of drinks. "I heard mention of a brother somewhere, but nobody's ever seen him."

"He died a few years ago," Kennedy Jones vouchsafed. "He was a civil servant in Africa."

"A civil servant? You've got to be kidding!"

"It's true. You'd never have taken them for brothers, though. They were opposites in everything."

"Which brother would *you* have gone for?" Jack asked Philippa, and then held up his hand. "No, don't tell me. I already know the answer!"

"Then you're wrong," she said equably. "I'm a hardboiled newspaper reporter. It would take more than a golden image to turn me on!"

"Meet our new adviser to the lovelorn," Kennedy Jones said disgustedly. "It's what a man is that matters, not what he has — yours sincerely, Aunt Tabitha!"

"Upon which note I'll make my goodbyes," Philippa smiled, "and leave you two to your gossip and booze."

Refusing their pleas to stay with them, she left them to their talk and walked the length of Fleet Street before deciding to look for a taxi. The cool air was welcome after the heat of the crowded bar, and she felt the sweat on her forehead evaporate and the stickinesss leave the nape of her neck.

Listening to gossip about Marius Lyon had in no way brought the man to life. Even knowing he had been hovering anxiously all day at the side of a hospital bed, the way Jessica Hibberd was doing now, did not give him the dimension of reality. This was not surprising; the magnitude of his power set him above the crowd. It must be lonely to be in such a position, she decided, and wondered who was lying so critically ill. A member of the family, Kennedy had said cryptically, but it could well be his diplomatic way of saying it was a girl-friend. A taxi drew in to the kerb and she climbed inside and gave the driver her address, forgetting Marius Lyon and everyone else as her thoughts returned to Cathy Joyce. If only she could find out what the girl had done.

For the rest of the week Philippa continued to supervise the "Dear Jessie" page, putting aside the few letters which she felt required the older woman's own kind of expertise. It was exhilarating to be in control and she marvelled that she could ever have considered turning down the job. It was a good thing Kennedy Jones had overridden her protests. She knew now what he had meant by saying that learning other people's problems would help her to become a better reporter. What he had meant — but had been too kind to say — was that she needed to become aware of suffering in order to appreciate and be grateful for her own uneventful life. There was nothing more conducive to soporific

27

writing than a sense of complacency.

She had grown up in an easy-going, cultured atmosphere, and her desire to be a reporter had been received with astonishment. Her father hoped that her stint on the local paper would help her to get the journalist bug out of her system, but success had only increased her desire to get to Fleet Street, and when she had finally managed to obtain a job with *Today's News* she had felt her career was just beginning.

Though accepting the fact that she lived alone in London and held down a job in one of the most hardboiled of all professions, her parents still treated her like a child when she returned home for the occasional weekend. It was gratifying to be cosseted and pampered, but equally pleasurable to leave the small manor house in Somerset and return to her cramped flat in Maida Vale. Two days of breakfast in bed, sherry at noon and the Bach cantatas on Sunday afternoon sent her hurrying back appreciatively to noisy streets and crowds.

Yet now, amidst the hurly-burly of a Friday afternoon, she longed for the quiet of her parents' home, and on an impulse telephoned them to say she would be coming down for the weekend.

When she returned to the office on Monday, it was to find Jessica Hibberd in charge again. Her husband was making good progress, and though he would be in hospital for a further month, he was off the danger list.

"It was wonderful to know you were in charge of everything," she told Philippa as they sipped their morning coffee. "With Frank so ill I couldn't have concentrated on anything."

"You didn't need to. I'm perfectly capable of coping. After all, it's what you've trained me to do."

"You need more than training to do this job. You need empathy."

"Don't you mean sympathy?"

"Empathy's more important. Sympathy can fool you into giving a sentimental answer, but empathy will help you to see things without it affecting your judgment."

Philippa was mulling over this when one of the messenger

boys came in with a letter. Anticipating it to be one that had been omitted from the postbag dumped in their office each morning, she was surprised to see the sudden rush of colour come into the older woman's face as she read the contents.

"Is anything wrong?" Philippa asked.

"I don't know. There must be, but I can't think what."

Unable to make head of tail of this reply, Philippa waited.

"It's from Marius Lyon," Jessica Hibberd went on. "He's sent me a cheque – for a quite staggering amount – and also my notice."

"*Your what*?" Phillippa asked, disbelievingly.

"He's fired me." The letter was picked up again and studied. "It's quite clear and to the point. My services are no longer required for the 'Dear Jessie' page, and I am reminded that the title belongs to the newspaper, and that under the terms of my agreement I cannot work on an advice column for any other national paper for the next three years."

"You can't have been fired!" Philippa was still incredulous. "There must be some mistake. Your page is one of the most popular features we have."

"There's no mistake about this cheque." Jessica Hibberd waved it in the air. "It's enough for me to retire on. Marius Lyon's making quite sure I won't have anything to complain about financially."

"But you can't let him fire you! It's a monstrous thing to do."

"He has the right, you know," the older woman said. "Though I do agree the whole thing is decidedly odd." She stood up. "No one's going to fire me without at least having the courtesy to tell me why."

Picking up her bag, she marched out, leaving Philippa to wonder at the working of the mind of the man who controlled this complex empire.

By the time she was ready to go to lunch, Jessica Hibberd had still not returned, and as she ate a cheese sandwich and munched on an apple, her thoughts were preoccupied and anxious. Long before she was due to return she went back to the office.

Jessica Hibberd was already at her desk, and though she still

29

looked flushed she seemed composed.

"Well," Philippa asked, "did you pull the lion's tail?"

"No one does that," Mrs. Hibberd said drily. "But I did get an apology. It was all a mistake."

Philippa sat at her own desk and waited to hear the rest. But nothing more was said, and the only sound that came from across the room was the clattering of the typewriter. Deciding regretfully that she was going to be told the reason for Marius Lyon's letter, nor why he had changed his mind, she set to work with her own letters.

Looking up as she debated an answer to one of them, she surprised Jessica Hibberd staring at her with such intensity that she could not overlook it. "Are you sure everything's all right?" she asked.

"Perfectly. It's just . . ." The woman pushed back her chair and went to stand by the window. "Did anyone come up to the office to see me while I was away? I'm not talking about this morning – I mean last week, when I was at the hospital?"

Philippa thought for a moment. "No one important or I'd have told you. There was the usual P.R.s, and someone from the Citizen's Advice Bureau. And there was also a man from some weird new religious movement."

"I was thinking of some of our readers. Did any of *them* call?"

"Not that I know of. Unless they saw Joan or Helen." Philippa named the other two assistants who worked on the column. "In fact there was hardly any – " She stopped as memory returned. "What an idiot I am! Someone did come to see you! A girl called Cathy Joyce. I couldn't get rid of her. She was so desperate to talk to someone that she never even gave me the chance to tell her I wasn't you."

"What happened?"

Philippa flushed. "I tried to get her to leave and write in to us, but she was in too much of a state to listen to me."

"What did she want?"

"Advice about her boy-friend."

"Which you gave her?"

30

"I'm afraid I did," Philippa said slowly, "and I've regretted it ever since."

"Why?" There was an unusual stillness in Jessica Hibberd's voice.

"Because – to quote something you said to me only this morning – I think my answer was based on sympathy rather than empathy. She wanted to elope, you see, and seemed awfully het-up at being under her uncle's thumb."

"And you told her that she *should* elope?"

"I said she was old enough to live her own life – that she should run off if she wanted to."

Mrs. Hibberd's voice was anguished. "I'm always telling you never to give such unequivocal answers!"

"I know," Philippa apologised, "and I was furious with myself afterwards. I tried to phone her, but I didn't have her address and I couldn't find it. I know you say we shouldn't give people a firm answer, but having her come up here like this – begging me to tell her what to do . . ."

"I can see it must have been hard for you." Mrs. Hibberd moved back to her chair. "Did she say anything more about herself?"

"Only that her boy-friend was a mechanic. It wasn't a question of his not beng able to afford to get married, so much as the step-mother and uncle not wanting her to get married at all."

"That's not surprising. She's barely eighteen."

"I know, but – " Philippa stopped, puzzled by what Mrs. Hibberd had just said. "How did you know she was eighteen? I didn't tell you her age."

"Marius Lyon did," Mrs. Hibberd said heavily. "Cathy Joyce Lyon is his niece."

For a long moment Philippa was speechless. How could the girl have been so deceitful! What audacity to come here in search of advice when she knew full well that her very position made it untenable for anyone working for Marius Lyon to proffer it. Slowly the shock ebbed, and as it did, she began to appreciate the desperation which had brought the girl here.

"I'll have to tell Mr. Lyon the truth," she said. "I suppose that's why he fired you. Because he thought *you* told his niece to elope."

"Yes."

"How did he find out she had been here?"

"She blurted it out when she was delirious." Seeing Philippa's surprise the woman continued: "She did take your advice, I'm afraid. That was how she got injured. She and her boy-friend were involved in a pile-up on the motorway. They were eloping to Gretna Green. The young man walked out of the accident scot-free, but Cathy was badly hurt."

So this was the girl for whom Marius Lyon had been keeping night and day vigil. Philippa expelled her breath in a long-drawn-out sigh. What an awful thing to happen! "I'm not surprised he was angry," she murmured.

"That's the understatement of the year!"

"What did he say when you told him it was me?"

"I didn't."

"You mean – ?"

"I didn't tell him who gave his niece the advice. First because I didn't know who it was until now, and secondly, because I'm technically responsible for any advice that comes from this page."

"You're not responsible for me," Philippa said bluntly, "and I won't let you take the blame for it."

"You can't apportion the blame in a manner like this. You weren't to know the elopement would end in tragedy."

"I should still have kept my mouth shut."

"It would have required someone with much more experience than you to have done that. If you've got someone begging you for advice, it's pretty hard to keep quiet."

"I'm still surprised Mr. Lyon didn't try and find out who was responsible," Philippa murmured.

"He may still try," Mrs. Hibberd said drily, "but I'll refuse to tell him."

"I think he has the right to know." Philippa stood up. "I'm going to see him."

"Don't be foolish," Mrs. Hibberd said with unexpected force. "I'm hoping you will take the column over when I leave, and if you tell him the part you played in his niece's elopement. . . ." Her voice trailed away as she saw the look on Philippa's face. "I *am* going to leave, my dear. It has nothing to do with Marius Lyon, though. I made up my mind when Frank was ill. I want to spend more time with him – travel perhaps. Even write the book I've always been promising myself I would."

"But you hadn't intended to leave yet?"

"I was giving myself three more months – until Frank was completely recovered from his operation. Then we were going to retire to the country and learn how to enjoy our leisure!" She motioned for Philippa to sit down. "When I got Mr. Lyon's letter this morning it was a terrible shock. After all, there's a world of difference in deciding to leave and in being summarily dismissed. That's why I was upset. But now things have been straightened out and – "

"Hardly that. Mr. Lyon still doesn't know the truth."

"There's no reason why he should. You can't blame yourself for Cathy Lyon's accident. Forget about it and think of the future."

"I couldn't write this column," Philippa muttered. "I haven't had the experience – Cathy alone proves that."

"She proves nothing! Now for goodness' sake stop thinking about yourself in defeatist terms. You're intelligent and a good writer. You won't find this page easy to do, but after three months you'll never want to give it up."

"Why can't you stay on and supervise?"

"Because the Aunt Jessie image needs changing. My ideas and standards don't fit today's trends. I've been realising that more and more. Even my reluctance to give firm answers is now outdated. This is the era of the expert – even the romantic expert – and readers want to be told what to do."

"Mollycoddling."

"Perhaps. But that's what is wanted. After all, we're a mollycoddled nation, what with our subsidies and free medicine and . . ." Mrs. Hibberd stopped and smiled. "Mr. Lyon would be furious if he heard me talk like this!"

Philippa did not reply, too involved with her own thoughts to give much attention to anyone else's. To run the "Dear Jessie" page would not only mean a greatly increased salary but also prestige, and though she might not wish to do it for more than a few years, it could lead to other more important assignments. Yet to accept what Mrs. Hibberd was so generously putting her way without completely exonerating the woman from blame over Cathy Lyon's accident was untenable. The prospect of seeing Marius Lyon and telling him the truth was frightening but less so than living with a bad conscience.

"I must tell him the truth," she averred.

Not giving herself a chance to change her mind, afraid that even a momentary hesitation would dissuade her from going, she ran out, heedless of Mrs. Hibberd's call to come back and talk it over.

It was not until she reached the top floor, where all the executive offices and directors were, that she realised she did not know the number of Marius Lyon's room. Slowing her pace, she looked at each door she passed, wondering how she could tell which one housed the big man himself. A girl of about her own age came out from a room on her left and Philippa hurried after her before she could disappear again.

"I'm looking for Mr. Lyon's office. Do you know where it is?"

"The double doors at the end of the corridor," the girl replied. "But you'd better knock on the other door beside it, that's Mrs. Brown's office."

Smiling her thanks, Philippa did as she was told, though Mrs. Brown's expression as she learned Philippa wanted to see Marius Lyon was a study in disbelief.

"Without an appointment? Even with one, you won't be able to see Mr. Lyon this week."

"I have to see him at once," Philippa reiterated. "It's terribly important."

"Perhaps you'd care to tell me what it's about?"

Philippa looked at the middle-aged secretary and sighed. She had as much chance of getting past Mrs. Brown as Aladdin would have had of entering the cave of treasure without the magic lamp. "It's about his niece, Cathy," she explained. "Mr.

Lyon saw Mrs. Hibberd a little while ago. But there's – there's something else he should know." Philippa's chin tilted. "I'm afraid I can't discuss it with you. It's confidential. But I do know that Mr. Lyon would want to see me if he knew what it was about."

Young flushed face stared into lined, powdered one.

"Very well," Mrs. Brown said, rising. "Please wait a moment . . ."

When the woman returned to her office she motioned silently to the door behind her; not that it would have made any difference if she had spoken, for Philippa's heart was thudding so loudly in her ears that she would not have heard her. This was her first sight of Marius Lyon. Pushing the hair away from her suddenly damp foreheard, she opened the door.

The lion's den, she thought in dismay, and stepped into it.

CHAPTER FOUR

The size of the room and the size of the man were two things Philippa noticed simultaneously. Both were large, over-powering and unexpected. Conservation of space, though preached by him, was not practised by him, and some hundred square yards of charcoal grey carpet lay beneath her feet. On it stood numerous leather armchairs and a vast satinwood table which acted as a desk. Its beautiful polished surface was covered with methodical piles of documents, together with several silver boxes and an inkstand the size of a small coffee tray. But the personality of Marius Lyon dwarfed the fittings. And not just his personality, she thought apprehensively, but the actual physical size of him.

He was well over six feet, with the build of a rugger player: massive shoulders and chest tapering down to a narrow waist. She had so frequently heard him referred to as the youngest newspaper tycoon in the country that she was surprised by the thick grey hair which swept back from his foreheard like a veri-table lion's mane. But the face beneath it was unlined, the skin tanned as though he spent more time out of doors than in his office which – from the amount of work he did – she knew to be untrue. Perhaps he had a sunlamp, she thought, and turned her eyes away from the narrow grey ones that were piercingly regarding her.

"Well?" His voice was as firm and strong as his appearance. "What's all this about you and my niece?"

Philippa moistened her lips and wished she had not rushed here so precipitately. Seeing the square, hard face staring at her, with its large dominant nose and wide mouth now set in a thin, tight line, she understood why Mrs. Hibberd had tried to pre-vent her. But it was too late to back out now; she was here and she must see it through.

"It wasn't Mrs. Hibberd who told your niece to – to get married. It was me."

"You!"

Philippa nodded and jerkily started to explain what had happened. But she had no chance to speak, for he angrily cut in on her.

"Who the hell gave you the right to tell a child of her age to run away and get married?"

"An eighteen-year-old isn't a child."

"That depends on the person. Cathy's a baby. Anyway, her age is irrelevant. What matters is the principle involved. You had no business to tell her – or anyone else for that matter – to defy their family. Jessica Hibberd's page is supposed to give commonsense advice, not encourage anarchy!"

Surprised by his illogical attack – for she could not see what anarchy had to do with the advice she had given his niece – she attempted to say so, but again he refused to hear her out, interrupting her with ever-increasing fury.

"The family unit is the one stable factor in today's society," he thundered. "Destroy that and you destroy everything!"

"If a family is united it can't be destroyed by other people's advice," she rejoined heatedly. "And I had no intention of destroying anyone when I told Cathy what to do."

"You should have kept quiet." His voice was louder still. "How dare you set yourself up as the arbiter of what anyone else should do?"

"We're paid to give advice!"

"You're paid to help people find their own solutions. And that doesn't mean turning their lives upside down! You got hold of my niece and acted as if you were God!"

"She was hysterical and desperate and I couldn't turn her away. I didn't want to give her advice, Mr. Lyon, but I had no choice."

"You shouldn't have seen her."

"She barged into the office before I could stop her."

"Then you should have sent her away."

37

"She wouldn't go. I tell you she was hysterical. She said if I didn't help her she would kill herself."

"Don't tell me you believed that rubbish?"

"You can't dismiss a threat of suicide as rubbish. If I've learned nothing else since I've been working for Mrs. Hibberd, I've at least learned that."

He flung his hands wide, as though conceding the point, but his anger was in no way appeased. "My niece's agitation makes your behaviour even less excusable, not more. If someone is hysterical the last thing you should do is to tell them to run off and get married."

"It was married or buried!" Philippa burst out. "That's what she said to me."

"And you believed her?"

"Enough not to take a chance on it. Anyway, I didn't tell her to elope. I merely said she was old enough to make up her own mind."

"You encouraged her to run off with that – " The man's hand clenched and banged on the desk with a thud that resounded through the room. "You should have been made to stay at Cathy's bedside the last two days. If you'd seen the results of your handiwork . . ."

He stopped speaking, his voice too thick with emotion, and Philippa stared at him, aghast at the unjustness of his accusation.

"You're entitled to think I shouldn't have spoken to your niece, but you can't blame me for the car crash."

"You were responsible for her elopement. If she hadn't run off with Alan she wouldn't be where she is now. I blame you totally!"

"Because it's easier than blaming yourself." Angered by his unfairness, her fear of him vanished. "It's ironic for you to talk about the value of a family unit. From what Cathy told me, there wasn't much unity in yours!"

"You know nothing about my family."

"I know that Cathy came to see a stranger because she couldn't talk to anyone else. That she has no respect for her stepmother and only fear for you!"

38

"How dare you talk to me like that!"

"Why shouldn't I?" Philippa cried. "You haven't cared what you've said to me!"

"Because it was your advice that put my niece in hospital – amost killed her."

"Your rigidity, you mean! If Cathy had been able to go to you with her problems she wouldn't have needed to go to a stranger. But she was scared to talk to you. She saw you as a dictator!"

"You know nothing of my relationship with my niece."

"I know what she told me."

"Do you always form an opinion on one-sided evidence?"

"You've formed an opinion of me without any evidence at all! I'm not surprised Cathy preferred to get help from the 'Dear Jessie' page."

"If you've quite finished. . . ."

"You don't like to hear the truth, do you?"

"Not your version of it. You're an interfering young woman whose meddling nearly cost Cathy her life."

"Haven't you heard one word I've said?" Philippa choked.

"And the sooner you leave my employ," he went on as if she had not spoken, "the better."

"You mean you're firing me?"

"Did you expect promotion?"

"I expected justice."

"From a rigid dictator?" he asked pointedly.

With an exclamation she ran to the door.

"You will have three months' severance pay," he called after her.

"Use it to buy yourself a whip," she retorted, and slammed the door behind her.

Jessica Hibberd knew better than to say "I told you so" when Philippa recounted the outcome of her meeting with Marius Lyon. Instead she offered to telephone the editor of a Sunday paper whom she knew was looking for a writer.

"Would you mind leaving it for a week?" Philippa pleaded. "Right now I'm so upset I don't want to see anybody about a job."

"Don't give up working on a paper because of Mr. Lyon."

"Don't worry about that." Memory of all he had said caused another explosion of anger. "If I were a man I'd have knocked him down!"

"He might have knocked you down first!"

"That wouldn't have surprised me. He's nothing but a bully. People of his type often are. They get to the top because they're willing to tramp over everyone who's in their way. I'm not surprised people hate him."

"Most people like him," Jessica Hibberd remonstrated. "Don't let anger blind you to the truth – the way it has with him."

The aptness of the comment helped to bridle Philippa's anger, and though it still simmered, it was no longer on the boil.

"You'd also be childish not to take the three months' pay," the older woman continued. "He won't know if you don't."

"I don't need his money," Philippa began to clear her drawers, dumping the contents of each one haphazardly on the desk and then bundling everything unceremoniously into a plastic carrier bag which she had found lying at the bottom of the cupboard where they kept their coats.

"I do wish you weren't going," Jessica Hibberd sighed. "I don't know what will happen to the page with both of us leaving so soon after each other."

"Perhaps Mr. Lyon will ask you to reconsider your decision," Philippa said.

"I doubt if he's ever asked anybody to reconsider anything in his life. He expects people to have the same devotion to the paper that he has, and if they don't, he'd never refer to it."

"What you mean," Philippa said scornfully, "is that he's willing to cut off his nose to spite his face."

"What you call obstinacy could equally well be called single-mindedness!"

"I'm in no mood to say anything nice about him."

"I don't blame you for being upset," Mrs. Hibberd said. "But don't get bitter about it."

40

"I won't. I've got more intelligence than to let Marius Lyon sour my life."

The words were more blithely said than meant, and during the next few days she found it difficult not to think of him without rancour. No matter how much she tried to see the situation from his point of view, she could not justify his fury towards her, nor his unreasonable refusal to admit that he himself was not blameless. Family unit, indeed! She tried to remember some of the things Cathy had said to her about him and her stepmother, but only vague words floated into her mind. How much more attentively she would have listened had she known that the uncle she had been referring to was the illustrious and despotic Marius Lyon!

At the end of the week Philippa went to see Jack Lane, having decided to try and get a job on her own initiative. Her confidence was justified, and when she left him after a short but pleasant interview, it was with the knowledge that she would be able to start work again on Monday. She was not well-known enough for her dismissal to have travelled along the Fleet Street grapevine, and though Jack Lane was surprised to see her, he assumed she was tired of working on an advice column and wanted to return to hard-core reporting.

"You'll find the atmosphere here quite different from Lyon Publications," he said, as he walked with her to the lift – not because he was being polite: journalists rarely were with each other – but because he was on his way to the compositors' room. "Once you're accepted in our group – and if you work well, you will be – then it's near enough a job for life; which is more than can be said for anyone who works for your ex-boss. He hires and fires people as often as I change my shirt!"

"It makes for bright papers."

"It also makes for ulcers."

"I don't think Mr. Lyon has any."

"The poor devils who work for him do!"

"Well, I'm a lucky devil who doesn't," she smiled, and was glad to step into the lift before she was encouraged to give an airing to the animosity she felt towards her ex-employer.

There was no doubt that Marius Lyon's personality was strongly etched on every newspaper and periodical he published. No writer or journalist who worked for him could ever sit back and relax on the assumption that having been there a long time they could regard their job as a sinecure. Always there were younger, highly ambitious people striving to dislodge them, and though this knowledge made for ulcers – as Jack Lane rightly said – it also made for bright, diamond-hard publications.

Philippa walked slowly down Fleet Street. There was an autumnal nip in the air and she decided to go home that weekend and take advantage of what could well be the last few warm days before winter. It would be good to see the beech trees before they finally shed their leaves. Their colour now would be the same colour as her hair. Automatically she pushed a heavy strand away from her cheek, and half-stopping to do so, caught herself reflected in a window. How tall and vibrant she looked; not even her monochrome reflection could diminish this, and she inexplicably thought of Cathy Joyce – Cathy Lyon as she now knew her to be – lying injured in some hospital ward. She tried to remember which hospital it was. Several came to mind, but she was not sure of the exact one. She began to walk again, and glimpsing a telephone kiosk, went in and dialled the Middlesex Hospital. Memory – though vague – was proved accurate, and she learned that Cathy Lyon was a private patient there, and doing as well as could be expected.

Putting down the telephone, Philippa continued on her way home, so immersed in the thought of her first and only meeting with the luckless girl that she found herself outside the entrance of Lyon Publications without realising she had made for it automatically.

"Talk about the power of suggestive thought," an amused voice said, and Philippa glanced round to see Jessica Hibberd beside her. "I've been ringing your flat all afternoon."

"I was with Jack Lane," Philippa explained. "I start working for him on Monday. But I'm on my way home now."

"Not just yet, you're not. You're coming to have a drink with me first."

Only when they were sipping coffee in a nearby café did the woman say why she had been trying to contact Philippa. "Cathy wants to see you."

"I just telephoned the hospital to find out how she was," Philippa said, "but I don't think it would be wise for me to visit her."

"She's very upset that you've been fired."

"Who told her?"

"Her uncle."

"He must have enjoyed doing that," Philippa said bitterly. "'I fired that interfering busybody who advised you to elope.' I can just hear him."

"You must be psychic," Mrs. Hibberd said drily. "Those were the very words he used!"

Philippa's anger firmed. What a hateful man he was! Even having his niece in hospital did not prevent him from gloating that her plans had been thwarted. What bad luck that the car had crashed. If it hadn't, the girl would already be married and free of his authority.

"She really does want to see you," Jessica Hibberd repeated. "That's why she called me. She didn't know how else to get in touch with you."

"It would be better if I didn't visit her," Philippa repeated. "Mr. Lyon would be furious if he found out."

"He won't know. And she's so anxious to see you."

"She'll forget me once she's out of hospital. They told me she was getting better and — "

"There are degrees of getting better," Mrs. Hibberd said, and her tone was so strained that Philippa looked at her sharply, knowing there was more to come.

When it did, she was so shocked she could not speak, and the guilt which had thought had receded rushed back with renewed force.

Cathy Lyon was unable to walk; unlikely ever to walk again.

"No wonder her uncle was so bitter," Philippa whispered.

"He didn't know about it then," Mrs. Hibberd replied. "The doctors believed it was bruising of the spine. Now they've discovered there's definite damage."

"Can't she move at all?"

"Not from the waist down. According to Cathy herself she should be a bit more mobile once the splints have been removed, but I'm not sure how true that is. The doctors might have told her that to pacify her."

"It's all my fault," Philippa burst out. "I'll never tell anyone what to do again – not even if they threaten to kill themselves in front of me!"

"You're blaming yourself for nothing," Jessica Hibberd was crisp and authoritative. "Cathy would have eloped with her boyfriend no matter what you said."

"But she mightn't have gone that night. It was raining and – "

"And she could just as easily have slipped on a wet pavement and broken her neck! For goodness' sake snap out of it."

"I can't."

"I think you would if you went to see her. She doesn't blame you for what happened. Her only concern is that you've been unjustly fired."

"She needn't worry about *that*."

"Tell her yourself. She'll keep ringing me till you do."

Philippa sighed. Much as she feared Marius Lyon's wrath if he discovered she had been to see his niece, she knew she would have no peace of mind until she went.

"I'll go and see her as soon as she's allowed visitors," Philippa said.

"If you say you're a member of the family they'll let you in whenever you want to go."

"I'll be a permanent resident there if Mr. Lyon arrives and finds me!"

"He's in America this week," Jessica Hibberd replied as they walked out of the café. "Why don't you go along tonight?"

"You mean I'll be safe?" Philippa asked ruefully.

"Marius Lyon's violence is never more than verbal!"

44

"I'll believe *that* so long as he's in America!"

A taxi cruised past, plying for hire, and seeing it as the beckoning hand of Fate, Philippa decided to take it. "I'll go and see Cathy now. I'll call you when I get back home."

"Don't forget. And leave your guilt complex in the hospital."

CHAPTER FIVE

Philippa's imagination, always vivid, clothed Cathy Lyon in a shroud of grief, and her first sight of the girl lying on a narrow hospital bed in no way made her revise her opinion. She was a travesty of the girl seen last week: pale as a lily, lifeless as a corpse she gave justification for her uncle's bitter anger, and for the first time some of Philippa's own anger towards the man ebbed. Having seen his niece like this, it was not surprising he had lashed out at her.

"I'm so glad you came," Cathy Lyon said weakly, and raised her hand. "I bet you never expected to see me like this."

"Accidents happen," Philippa was aware of the inadequacy of her answer. "But I hear you're making splendid progress."

"Then you must have better hearing than me! I'm not making any progress at all."

"That's not true. Only a few days ago you were on the danger list and now you're allowed visitors – otherwise I wouldn't be here."

"Do you call that getting better? The doctors say it will be a couple of years before I can walk again."

"Doctors aren't infallible."

"These are," Cathy said. "My uncle only has the best."

"Then show your uncle that he can sometimes be wrong – make up your mind to walk in *one* year! You've got to try, Cathy. You can't lie here feeling sorry for yourself."

"You'd feel sorry if you were me," Cathy said sulkily. "I thought you'd be more sympathetic."

Holding her sympathy in check, Philippa said: "You're alive and you're going to get better, so why do you need sympathy?"

The girl coloured angrily, the pinkness apparent on her pale cheeks. "I always knew journalists were tough. You're just like my uncle."

Philippa felt a momentary triumph. To have come here and

46

commiserated with her would have been the worst thing possible. "You didn't think I was tough the night you came and asked me for advice."

"I thought you were Mrs. Hibberd. You should have told me you weren't."

"You didn't give me a chance. Anyway, I was her assistant."

Cathy reacted at once to the use of the past tense. "That's why I wanted to see you. I'm sorry my uncle fired you. He had no right to do that, and I told him so."

"You shouldn't have done," Philippa said tremulously. "If you hadn't listened to me that night you wouldn't be here now."

"I would have run away with Alan no matter what you had said. I only wanted confirmation. If you hadn't given it to me I'd have thought you were like everyone else – prejudiced against Alan because he's poor."

"If I'd known how rich *you* were," Philippa said drily, "I would probably have given you different advice."

"There!" Cathy was sulky again. "I knew you'd say that. Just because Alan has to work for a living and can't afford – "

"I wasn't thinking of your boy-friend's financial position," Philippa interrupted. "Merely that I'd have thought more carefully about yours. Rich girls of eighteen have a different outlook from poor ones."

"I wasn't brought up as an heiress. Until I came to live with my uncle my background was quite ordinary. My father never accepted any financial help from Marius and they were quite different in their outlook. Daddy was gentle and unworldly and – well, you know what my uncle's like."

"A clever man," Philippa said tactfully, and moved away to sit in a chair by the window. "How long will you have to stay in hospital?"

"What difference does it make? I'm a prisoner whether I'm here or at home."

"You shouldn't say a thing like that."

"It's true. I suppose you know my uncle won't let me see Alan?"

"I hadn't heard that," Philippa admitted.

47

"Well, he won't." The dark head moved restlessly on the pillow though the body remained supine. "Would you like to know how I met him?"

Aware that Cathy wished to talk about her boy-friend – as though doing so would make his presence felt – Philippa nodded, and the gesture unleashed a torrent of words. It was the kind of story one might have read in an old-fashioned magazine, and it was hard to believe such events could occur in the present day. Yet facts were often stranger than fiction and the facts, as Cathy presented them, illustrated this. Her life had been uneventful until her mother had died when she was twelve. The next two years she had drawn close to her father, and it was a closeness which had not changed when – on holiday in Durban – he had met Celia Maddon, married her within a week of their meeting and brought her back to Nairobi as his wife. Marriage had not changed the tenor of Arthur Lyon's household, and life had gone on in the same way. Whether this would have continued was a matter of conjecture, for within three months he had died of a heart attack. At the funeral Celia met her brother-in-law for the first time, and Marius, impressed by her quiet grief and the coolly efficient way she controlled a tempestuous and heart-broken fourteen-year-old girl, had immediately offered her the hospitality of his home until she decided where and how she wanted to live.

"That was four years ago," Cathy said, "and Celia hasn't decided yet! Marius is too stupid to see she doesn't ever intend to leave. She's going to make it permanent."

"How?"

"By marrying him."

"Would you mind?"

"I couldn't care less. They deserve each other. He's a hot-tempered bully and she's an ice-cold bitch!"

"You're exaggerating," Philippa said halfheartedly.

"I'm under-estimating," Cathy frowned, "at least as far as Celia's concerned. Much as I don't like my uncle, I think he's too good for her. I'm sure she's the one who's turned him against Alan."

48

"You still haven't told me about him," Philippa intervened determinedly, fighting her curiosity to learn more of Marius Lyon and the blonde Celia.

But there wasn't, it seemed, all that much to tell. Alan was twenty-four, his parents lived in Liverpool but he lived in London. A mechanic by trade, his hobby was motor-racing, and it was at Brands Hatch – where Cathy had gone with some friends one Saturday afternoon – that she had met him. They had immediately been attracted to one another, and unsuspecting that her friendship with him would meet with family disapproval, she had invited him home.

"For the first few weeks Marius said nothing about it," Cathy went on. "But one evening he called me into his study and said he didn't want me to see Alan again. He said I was too young to know my own mind and that Alan only wanted to marry me because I was his niece."

"Did he have any specific reason for saying that?"

"My uncle never needs a reason for what he says or does. The minute he thinks something, it becomes a fact!"

"Surely he must have based what he said on something other than instinct," Philippa persisted.

"It was Celia," Cathy said solemnly. "She disliked Alan the minute she met him. She knew that if I married him she'd have no more reason to stay on in the house."

Cathy was repeating what she had said to Philippa the first time they met, and as before, there was no way of knowing how true it was. If Celia was intent on becoming Marius Lyon's wife she would undoubtedly discourage anything that might send her out of his orbit. Yet surely, having lived in his home for four years, her position was already secure?

"No one's secure in my uncle's life," Cathy answered, as Philippa asked the question aloud. "He's not the sort of man a woman can ever be sure of. Celia was scared that if I married Alan, Marius would ask her to find a place of her own. You can imagine how happy she is knowing I'm going to be stuck in a wheelchair for the next few years. It should give her more than enough time to rope and tie my uncle."

49

"From what you've told me about him, I shouldn't think it will be all that easy."

"He's very nice to her," the younger girl said grudgingly.

"Perhaps if they did get married they'd be more understanding about you and Alan."

Cathy's face brightened. It was a thought which had not struck her before and she gave Philippa a questioning look. "At the moment I can't figure out how I'm going to see Alan, let alone marry him. My uncle's forbidden him to come to the house, and as I'm stuck in a wheelchair . . . Hell!" she burst out suddenly.

"Hardly as bad as that," Philippa ventured carefully. "Don't you think your uncle might change his mind in a few weeks? Once he sees you are getting better and his temper's had a chance to cool down. . . . I mean, he was very upset when you eloped."

"He has no reason to be upset. If he didn't see everything in terms of money, he wouldn't be so cynical. He can't believe anyone can love me because I'm me."

"I'm sure that's not true."

"It is!" Cathy cried. "He said so. He was hateful about Alan. I've already told you. That's why we decided to run away – to show my uncle we were going to get married whether he gave his consent or not." The thin voice trembled. "And now I can't even *see* Alan. Even my phone calls are monitored." She burst into sobs, and afraid that a nurse might hear and come in, Philippa hurried across to placate her.

"Please don't cry," she begged. "You're just playing into your uncle's hands if you do. If you and Alan love each other, you've got to prove it."

"How?" Cathy gulped.

"By showing that even though you can't meet, you won't change your minds. After a few months I'm sure – "

"A few months!" Cathy wailed, and cried even louder.

This time the noise did bring in a nurse, who flung Philippa a look of stony disapproval as she flicked a watch out of her breast pocket and grasped Cathy's wrist between finger and thumb.

"No more visitors," she said briskly. "They make you too excited."

"I'm not excited." Cathy made an effort to stem her tears and looked beseechingly at Philippa. "Please stay."

"I've already been here too long."

"But you're the only person I can talk to. Promise you'll come and see me again?"

"Very well," said Philippa, hiding her reluctance.

"Tomorrow?"

"Next week."

"Give me your phone number," Cathy replied. "Then I can nag you."

With a slight smile Philippa gave it to her and then left, but sitting on the bus as it jogged down Oxford Street, she vowed not to become involved in the girl's affairs. On the face of it, Marius Lyon's refusal to countenance his niece's engagement seemed high-handed, but he could well have a good reason for objecting to Alan – apart from the one he gave to Cathy. Even the objections of the unknown Celia could be valid. After all, she only had Cathy's opinion of Alan on which to form her own, and bearing in mind the girl's love of dramatization, everything she said had to be taken with a large pinch of salt. But the problem of Alan, and whether he was or wasn't a suitable young man, was not something with which she intended to concern herself. She had done so once already, and lost an enjoyable job because of it, and she had no intention of doing so again. Let the Lyon family look after themselves!

However, her resolve to do this was destroyed by Cathy, who telephoned early the next morning and begged her to come and visit her that day. So pleading was she that Philippa was unable to refuse, and three o'clock that afternoon found her once more by the girl's bedside.

This second visit was less traumatic than the first one. Having already spoken at length about her stepmother and uncle, Cathy seemed content to discuss generalities and displayed particular interest in the work Philippa had done on the "Dear Jessie" page.

51

"It was unfair of Marius to fire you," she said suddenly. "I'm going to ask him to give you back your job."

"You'll do no such thing. I wouldn't work for your uncle if – " She stopped too late, for Cathy was looking at her speculatively.

"Was he awfully rude to you?"

"He wasn't polite."

"I suppose he blamed you completely for the accident?"

"It doesn't matter now," Philippa said quickly. "I'm starting another job on Monday, so there's no need for you to feel guilty."

"But you loved working on the 'Dear Jessie' page. You just said so."

"That doesn't mean I wanted to stay there for ever. As a matter of fact I needed a change. Now let's talk about something else."

With unexpected docility Cathy complied. When not displaying resentment against her family she had a gay manner that made her easy to like. She had a quick wit too and was an excellent mimic. All in all, a delightful girl, Philippa thought as she left, having promised to return the following day.

With Marius Lyon still in America, she had no fear of meeting him accidentally at the hospital, though she knew that once he returned to England she would have to plan her visits more carefully. Not that would have much free time after this week was over; starting a new job was always nerve-racking, and Jack Lane's terms of engagement had been so vague that she had no clear idea what he intended her to do.

"Everything" seemed to be the most suitable word to describe her first three days on *The Monitor*. She covered a fashion show for the regular fashion writer who was away ill, interviewed a pop star who had sold his first million records, and took a quick trip to Brighton to see a medium who claimed to be in touch with the spirit of Karl Marx. Only her interview with the pop star appeared in the paper, and even this was ruthlessly cut by half, a fate that befell many feature writers, though Philippa, used to being Jessica Hibberd's assistant where nothing she wrote had been cut without reference back to her, found this occurrence particularly galling.

52

But her frustration disappeared when – going to see Cathy early on Wednesday evening – she found the girl sitting in a completely upright position, and looking considerably better than she had expected. How trivial one's work problems were when compared with one's health and well-being.

"You look a hundred per cent better than you did the first time I was here," she said truthfully.

"I feel better. The physiotherapist is terribly pleased with me."

"I'm sure they'll soon have you walking out of here."

"Not quite," Cathy smiled, "but they aren't making me stay flat on my back for hours at a time. I can sit up as much as I like."

"You must be very pleased with yourself."

"You're the one who should be pleased," Cathy replied.

"Why me?" Philippa asked, surprised.

"Because your visits each day have stopped me dying of boredom. You're the first friend I've ever had of my own age. In Kenya I didn't have any at all and since coming to live with Marius I've just had a lot of hangers-on because of his money and who he is."

"Poor little rich girl," Philippa teased.

"I am now." Bitterness flitted across the delicate features. "But I won't be for long. I'm going to walk before those two years are up, Philippa. I feel it in my bones. And once I can stand on my own feet. . . ." Cathy shook her head as though unwilling to put the rest of her thoughts into words. "But don't let's talk about me any more. Tell me how you're settling down in your new job."

Philippa launched into an amusing but monitored account of the past three days, adding a large dollop of imagination to each of her assignments, so that she had Cathy in helpless laughter over her interview with the pop star, and in goggle-eyed amazement at her re-enactment of her visit to the medium.

"I've often wondered whether it's possible to get in touch with the spirit world," Cathy murmured.

"Are you sure it even exists?"

53

"I'd like it to. I know my uncle thinks it's a load of nonsense. I once heard him talking to Celia about voodoo. He couldn't have been more sceptical if he'd tried."

Philippa could well imagine what he must have said. A man like Marius Lyon, who believed so implicitly in his own power and strength, would never be able to credit something he could not see with his own eyes, or which he could not logically work out in his own mind. Not for him the jump in the dark that might lead to a great discovery or shattering truth; all his facts had to be verified; all his beliefs to be substantiated.

"I think Alan believes in spirits," Cathy's voice interrupted Philippa's reverie. "At least he wears a good luck charm. He says he'd never race without it. He's always talking about having the luck of the devil."

"He must have," Philippa could not forbear saying, "to have walked away from the crash without a scratch."

"That wasn't his fault," Cathy said quickly. "He would much rather have been in hospital than me. He said so."

"I'm sure he meant it," Philippa said hastily. "But I thought your uncle had forbidden you to see him."

"He can't forbid me," Cathy said, unexpectedly sullen. "I've reached the age of consent, remember. All he's done is made it impossible for us to meet while I'm in hospital. But Alan rang me one night. He managed to get past the switchboard. He hasn't succeeded in doing it again, though. I expect Marius gets recordings of everyone who calls me."

"Aren't you exaggerating what your uncle does? I'm sure it isn't good for you to build him up into the demon king!"

"He doesn't need any build-up," Cathy retorted. "He *is* a demon!"

"He's been very good to you since your father died," Philippa remonstrated. "From what you've told me he's given you everything you've wanted – and your stepmother too."

"Marius can be marvellous so long as you do everything he wants, but the moment you try and cross him. . . . His trouble is that he thinks he knows more than anyone else."

Unwilling to enter into a discussion concerning her erstwhile

54

employer, Philippa tried to change the subject. But Cathy was not to be dissuaded. Marius and Alan were uppermost in her mind and Marius and Alan were the two men she wanted to talk about.

"While I'm ill, I've got no choice but to obey him," she admitted. "But that won't stop me from seeing Alan. I'll manage it even if I have to crawl out of the house on my hands and knees!"

"I'm sure your uncle will let you see him," Philippa pacified. "If you can make him realise that you and Alan are really in love – that it isn't infatuation – I'm sure he'll – "

"Do you think I haven't tried?" Cathy burst out. "But nothing will convince him I know my own mind. He still thinks of me as a child – he said so. 'You're an innocent baby.' Those were his exact words."

"He probably still regards you as the fourteen-year-old who first came to live with him. It's often difficult for adults to realise that children don't remain children for ever."

Unexpectedly Cathy giggled. She was prone to swift changes of mood which, in fact, made Philippa wonder if her uncle's assessment of her might not be right after all. The thought was disquieting; the last thing in the world she wanted was to find herself in the position of agreeing with Marius Lyon.

"Why are you giggling?"

"Because of the way you referred to Marius as a grown-up – as if you and I are kids."

"He made me feel like one," Philippa confessed wryly.

"That's because he lost his temper with you," Cathy said bluntly. "But when he puts on the charm he can make you feel like the Queen of Sheba."

Doubting both his charm and his ability to make her feel like the Queen of Sheba, Philippa nonetheless refrained from comment.

"Were you rude to him too?" Cathy was speaking again. "You never did tell me what you said when you had that row."

"It's unimportant."

"You're not still scared of him, are you?"

"Why on earth should I be? He's nothing in my life any more, and he can't get me fired from my present job."

"I'd put nothing past him," Cathy said darkly.

"Don't be silly. One benefit of being a member of a union is that Machiavellian employers can have their claws clipped!"

"Then how would you feel about doing something that might – " Cathy hesitated, "that might annoy him if he found out? Not that he need ever know about it, of course. It's just that – well, you know what I mean."

"I'm not sure I do," Philippa lied, knowing full well what was coming.

"I'd like you to go and see Alan for me," came the blunt request. "If we had a sort of go-between, it would help us to feel closer."

"I was once asked to play the nurse in *Romeo and Juliet*," Philippa said drily, "but I turned it down. It wasn't a role in which I fancied myself."

"We're not asking you to help us plot another elopement. I couldn't rush away with Alan while I still need expensive treatment. It's just that if I knew you had seen him – if you could tell him personally how I am, and then come back and tell me how *he* is – '

Tears shone in the large dark eyes and Philippa could not help but be moved by them. Against her better judgment she found herself agreeing to what was being asked of her, and when she left the hospital it was with Alan's address in her handbag and a promise to phone him that evening.

As she turned the key in her front door she heard the telephone ring, and a premonition that it might be Alan himself thankfully died as she lifted the receiver and heard Jessica Hibberd's voice.

"Jack Lane must be working you overtime," the woman grumbled good-naturedly. "This is the second night I've tried to reach you."

"Don't blame Jack. I've been going to see Cathy straight from work."

"Cathy Lyon?"

"You sound surprised," Philippa replied. "If it hadn't been for you I wouldn't have gone in the first place."

"I wanted you to see her to put your conscience at rest; not to become her guide and mentor."

"What makes you think I am?"

"I have a feeling in my old bones." There was silence and when it had lengthened appreciably, Mrs. Hibberd spoke again. "I can see my old bones are right. I was hoping you might have disclaimed what I said."

"Cathy's got no one to turn to," Philippa admitted slowly.

"She has a host of people at her beck and call. Don't let her batten on to you."

"I won't."

"You mean she hasn't yet asked you to act as go-between for her and her boy-friend?"

Philippa's intake of breath supplied its own answer, and Mrs. Hibberd gave a snort of exasperation. "Really, Philippa, don't you know better than to get so involved in other people's affairs?"

"*You* should talk!" Philippa retorted.

"At least *I've* got the experience of old age. *You* do it without thinking."

"I know," Philippa said bitterly. "That's why Cathy will be in a wheelchair for the next two years."

This time it was Jessica Hibberd who caught her breath. "So you still feel guilty. I was hoping you didn't."

"It isn't a question of guilt. It's just that I like Cathy and I think she likes me. If seeing her can be a help, then I can't refuse."

There was another pause. "Tell me what she's like. I've only spoken to her on the telephone."

"She's nothing like her uncle. She's slight and dark – a bit like an elf. Not much of a figure, and a narrow, peaky face. She's got a breathless way of talking, and one minute she acts like an adult and the next like a kid."

"You certainly seem to have studied her," Jessica Hibberd said drily. "That's the most alive description I've heard you

57

give of anybody. You make her sound like a cross between Alice in Wonderland and Snow White!"

"At the moment she's more like Snow White," Philippa admitted.

"And which little dwarf are you?"

"I know which one *you* are," Philippa teased. "Nosey!"

"All right, so I *am* nosey. But you can't blame me. After all, I was the one who made you go and see Cathy in the hospital, and if you're going to get involved in her life then I – "

"I was involved from the minute I opened my mouth and told her what to do. Nothing you say can alter the way I feel about that. I'm in it up to my neck."

"Let me know before it rises above your head," Mrs. Hibberd said, "and I'll throw you a lifebelt."

"I'll remember the offer," Philippa replied, and deliberately changed the subject to enquire after Frank Hibberd's progress.

When she finally put down the receiver, she stood beside it indecisively, knowing that unless she rang Alan Bedford now she might lack the courage to do it later. With a sigh she dialled his number, and hearing it ring several times, was about to thankfully hang up when he came on the line. He seemed surprised when he learned who was calling him, and there was unmistakable reserve in his voice, as though he was unsure if the call was a trap. But as she went on talking to him about Cathy his tone changed, and before the call ended she found herself inviting him over to join her for coffee.

Like it or not, she had forged herself into a link between two unhappy young lovers, and she prayed to heaven that this second intervention on her part would not end as tragically as the first.

CHAPTER SIX

Cathy had given no description of Alan, and Philippa was unprepared for the slim, fair-haired young man who presented himself at her front door at nine o'clock that evening. He settled himself easily into an armchair and chatted to her as if he had known her for years, taking it for granted that she was completely on his side.

"I think there's a great advantage in being Swedish or Swiss," she said firmly, during a momentary lull in his conversation. "They're always neutral," she added, seeing his blank look.

Immediately he knew what she meant, though he did not appear to be disconcerted by it. "Even neutrals can have a point of view. After all, sitting on the fence they probably see things in a less biased way!"

"But they still remain neutral – like the three wise monkeys." He looked blank and she added: " 'Speak no evil, see no evil, hear no evil.' "

"Surely there's nothing evil about Cathy and me wanting to get married?" he protested. "And you can't blame me for the accident, the way her uncle does. When I opened my eyes and saw her pinned under the car – with me thrown completely clear – I'd have given ten years of my life to have changed places with her."

"I'm sure she'll get well," Philippa soothed, perturbed by the distress that cast a veil of perspiration over his small, well-cut features.

"Can anyone be sure?" he burst out. "Have you spoken to her doctors?"

"No, I haven't. I get the news from Cathy."

"Then heaven knows what the truth is! I'm sure they won't tell her if she's going to be a cripple for life."

"You mustn't think like that." Philippa was shocked. "She's

59

so much better than she was. Even in the last few days she's a different person."

"How would I know?" he said bitterly. "They won't let me near her."

"Have you tried to talk to Mr. Lyon?"

"It would be easier to talk to the Dalai Lama! But one day I'll *make* him talk to me – you mark my words."

Philippa's scalp tingled apprehensively. "You're not planning to do anything foolish, are you?"

"Not unless you think it's foolish of me to want to marry Cathy?"

"I didn't mean that."

"What did you mean, then?"

Deciding his blunt question merited an equally blunt reply, she said: "Cathy's in no state – either mentally or physically – to get married to anyone at the moment. She needs rest and treatment."

"You don't need to tell me that." He jumped to his feet and paced the room. "She needs everything I can't afford to give her – care, attention, the best doctors, the best physiotherapists. All the things that Marius Lyon's money can buy. The only thing he can't buy her is happiness! I'm the only one who can give her that." He swung round and peered at Philippa, his light brown eyes searching. "You do agree with me, don't you?"

"I don't know you well enough to agree or disagree," she said carefully.

"But you asked me to come here . . . to talk about Cathy. You can't be against us!"

"I'm neutral," she reaffirmed. "And I want Cathy to remain as calm as possible. That's the only reason I agreed to see you: to stop Cathy from getting upset."

Alan put his hands in the pockets of his trousers and teetered thoughtfully on his heels. "You're honest," he said slowly. "I'll say that much for you."

"Thanks!"

"No, I mean it. Don't get me wrong."

She did not reply and he wandered idly around the room,

looking at her books – classical novels and contemporary biographies – and at her pictures: an original oil she had picked up along the Bayswater Road and some delicate watercolours which had been a twenty-first birthday present from her parents. Not sure if he was trying to calm himself, she waited and watched him.

"You're not as I imagined," he said suddenly. "I thought you'd be older and more hard-faced!"

"Every man's idea of a woman reporter," she quipped. "I'm sorry to disappoint you."

"It's no disappointment." He came to stand beside her. "You're very good-looking."

She was too used to compliments to blush – one good thing about working in Fleet Street, she thought, and gave Alan the battery of her sherry-gold eyes. If he was a flirt she might as well find out now and advise Cathy accordingly.

His own eyes, pale blue and intent, stared back at her, but there was no flirtatious gleam in them, merely frank appraisal and interest, so that she relaxed and motioned him to sit down again. He did so, boyishly flinging one leg over the arm of the chair, an attitude which made him look younger than the twenty-six she knew him to be.

"Do you think I'm after Cathy's money?" he asked laconically.

"I don't know. Are you?"

"She hasn't got any. It's always been a matter of conjecture whether or not her uncle would go on keeping her in the style to which he's made her accustomed!"

"He certainly wouldn't if she married someone he didn't approve of."

"Then I've answered your question, haven't I?" he said. "Because Mr. King-of-the-Jungle-Lyon doesn't approve of *me*, and if Cathy and I got married she'd have to live on *my* salary."

The statement made Philippa wonder again why Marius Lyon disapproved of Alan Bedford. Was it solely because of his lack of money or was there another, more basic reason? Well-mannered though he was, Alan Bedford obviously came from a working-class background, which might not fit in with

61

Marius Lyon's preconceived ideas of an acceptable suitor for his niece. Not that the newspaper tycoon himself heralded from a moneyed or landed background. But then people who came up the hard way were often bigger snobs than true aristocrats.

"If you and Cathy did eventually get married," she ventured, "and her uncle still refused to – "

"We'd manage," Alan intervened. "I can't keep her in diamonds, but she wouldn't be on the breadline! I'm in charge of a garage in North London," he added. "There's nothing I don't know about cars."

"Such modesty!"

"It doesn't pay to be modest."

"I hear you go racing too."

"It's my hobby. But I'm more interested in developing cars for racing. Improving the performance of the engine – things like that."

"You make it sound as if there are problems about doing it."

"There are. It requires money. If I had the proper backing I could produce a winning car in six months. But as it is. . . ." He shrugged. "I race a bit instead. It gives me extra cash and lots of girls. You've no idea how popular racing drivers are."

"You'd better not let Cathy hear you!"

"I'm talking about my past," he joked. "After I met Cathy there was no one else for me. But I met *her* on the track. She came down with a crowd of Guards officers. If it hadn't been for my racing we'd never have met. Socially we're light-years apart." Again he roamed the room, fidgeting with various ornaments. "What are my chances of getting to see her?"

"Non-existent, unless you get Mr. Lyon's approval. You might be able to sneak in while she's still in hospital, but once she's home you won't stand a chance."

"Then what can I do?"

"I don't know. Are you sure he won't talk to you?"

"Positive." He came to stand in front of Philippa. "What are the chances of *your* persuading our noble Lyon to change his mind?"

"Even less than yours. He dislikes me as much as he dislikes you."

Alan shook his head. "That sounds wrong to me. From what I heard, he's got an eye for pretty girls."

"Not the ones he's fired," Philippa said crisply, and stood up. The evening had gone on long enough. She had promised Cathy to see Alan and she had done so. To let the meeting reach the stage where she might be co-opted to aid and abet their plans was definitely not on the agenda.

Aware of what was in her mind, Alan picked up his leather jacket and slung it over his shoulders before moving to the door. It gave him an air of masculinity that added strength to his delicately moulded features, and she could understand why Cathy had fallen in love with him. He was not the type to appeal to herself, though. She needed someone with more strength; a more dominating personality.

Hurriedly she moved to the door. "Any special message you want me to give Cathy?"

"Tell her I love her, and that she's to get well quickly."

"I think the first part of your message will help the second part to come true."

"I hope so," he said soberly, and with a wave of his hand walked down the hall.

Knowing Cathy would be eager for news of Alan, Philippa went to see her during her lunch break the next day. Luckily it was Friday, which meant the main Saturday features had gone to press on Thursday night. Her own article, the first carrying her by-line, was due to appear in the paper on Monday, and it lay on her desk awaiting her final revision.

Unwilling to be away too long, she took a taxi to the hospital and, ignoring the lift, raced up the stairs to the second floor and Cathy's room. Only as she opened the door and stepped breathlessly inside did she realise Cathy was not alone. A burly figure half-blocked the light coming from the window.

The colour drained from her face and she stood rooted to the spot. What an idiot she was not to have remembered that Marius Lyon was due home today! Obviously the first thing he had done was to come and see his niece. She looked at Cathy and moistened her lips.

"I'll come back later. I didn't know you – "

"Don't go on my account." Marius Lyon's voice was loud in the small room. "Sit down."

Nervously Philippa did so, and only as she took the weight off her feet did she realise she was trembling. She was crazy to let this man's presence affect her like this. He meant nothing in her life and she had no reason to be frightened of him. Yet she was terribly conscious of his pure physical bulk: his broad shoulders, his leonine head and the light-footed yet menacing tread as he moved from the window to the bed and back to the window again, as if he found the smallness of the room too confining. A lion in a cage, she thought involuntarily, and turned her head away from him.

"Philippa works for *The Monitor* now," Cathy said, cutting across her uncle's recounting of a meeting he had had with an American senator.

He stopped in mid-sentence and glanced at Philippa before looking back at his niece. "There's no shortage of jobs in Fleet Street for good writers."

"So you admit Philippa was good, do you?"

"She must have been or Kennedy Jones wouldn't have employed her!"

"*You* employed her," said Cathy.

"Indirectly."

"But you sacked her directly!"

Philippa's cheeks flamed. "Cathy, please – "

"Why shouldn't I say it?" Cathy demanded. "You've no reason to be embarrassed by what happened. My uncle isn't."

"I am never embarrassed by my own actions," he remarked, his deep voice devoid of inflection.

"Because you don't care about people." Quick tears glittered in Cathy's eyes.

"I care about you," he said, and came to the bed to rest a large hand on the crown of the dark head.

It was an unexpectedly tender gesture and Philippa watched

fascinated as he continued to stroke the long strands of hair, speaking to Cathy in the quiet tones one would use to a high-spirited filly.

"You've improved wonderfully while I've been away. You're almost back to normal. The doctors say you should be able to come home next week."

"I'd rather stay here," Cathy muttered. "I hate my bedroom at home."

"It's been redecorated for you."

The pale face tilted up towards him, transformed. "Oh, Marius, how kind you are! You've no idea how much I hated that mahogany furniture."

"I should have," he said whimsically. "You went on about it often enough."

"Only because you refused to let me change it." She caught his hand and rubbed it against her cheek. "Have you got me the brass fourposter and the William Morris wallpaper?"

"Everything's the way you wanted it. It's complete Art Nouveau, from Tiffany lampshade to Turkey carpet." The grey head tilted in Philippa's direction. "From our conversation you will have deduced that Cathy is no lover of the Georgian or Regency period."

Since Philippa herself was, and found the thought of Tiffany lampshades and Turkey carpet appalling, she gave a murmur which she hoped was non-committal.

The man turned back to the bed. "I'm sure you have girlish gossip to exchange with Miss – " He hesitated, obviously unable to remember Philippa's second name, and then said easily: "I'll be in to see you later tonight. It will be early though, because I'm dining at Number 10."

"Telling the Prime Minister how to run the country?"

"I'm sure you'd rather I did that than tell you how to run your life!"

"I have no life for you to run now."

Once more Cathy was sullen, her good humour gone. With a shrug Marius Lyon went to the door, nodded in Philippa's direction and went out.

Hardly had the door closed behind him when Cathy flung out her arms to Philippa. "What did Alan say? Did he give you a message for me? How did he look? You did see him last night, didn't you?"

"Yes, I did, and he looks fine." Glancing apprehensively over her shoulder as though to make sure the door was firmly closed, Philippa recounted her meeting with Alan, forced by Cathy's insistence to try and remember every single word they had spoken.

"You make it seem as if he's in the room with you." Tears poured down Cathy's face and flags of excited red glowed in her cheeks. "You're a wonderful story-teller, Philippa."

"I'm not telling a story," Philippa chided. "It's the truth."

"And you think he still loves me?"

"Of course he does."

"Did you tell him I still love him?"

"He didn't think it necessary to ask such a silly question." Philippa glanced at her watch and stood up. "I must go. I only popped in to see you because I know you'd be anxious to hear what happened."

"Will you come back tonight?"

"I've no intention of repeating the whole story," Philippa said, shaking her head.

"When are you seeing Alan again?"

The question made Philippa realise the difficulty of her position. Having agreed to meet Alan once, it was going to be impossible not to do so again. Yet this was exactly what she did not want to do. "We've made no arrangements to meet. I think the next thing is for you to tackle your uncle."

"It's no use. He'll never let me see him."

Cathy burst into noisy sobs. It was unexpected and discomfiting, and Philippa ran over and caught her close. "Don't cry, darling. I'm sure things will work out for you. It's just a matter of time. If you could only learn to control your temper with your uncle, I'm sure you could talk him into letting you see Alan."

"I try not to lose my temper," Cathy hiccoughed, "but I

can't help it. I talk before I think. That's always been my trouble."

"At least you know your faults," said Philippa, trying to inject some humour into the conversation. "That's halfway to changing them." She handed the girl a Kleenex and waited till the tears had completely stopped before picking up her handbag and moving to the door. "If I don't get back to the office soon, I'll be fired."

"Will you come and see me tomorrow?"

"I'm not sure. Now your uncle's back I – "

"He knows I've been seeing you. You're not to stop coming because of him." Again tears looked imminent, and hastily Philippa nodded and hurried out.

In the corridor she paused and drew a deep breath. She was still shaking with nerves and was surprised to find her skin damp. She was reacting to Marius Lyon in as childish a manner as Cathy. It was incredible that a mere man – albeit a rich and important one – should make her feel like this.

Bracing her shoulders, she went in search of a cloakroom, where she washed her face and muted the colour of her flushed cheeks with powder. She stared at herself in the mirror: what a sight she looked! If only she had had the foresight to make herself tidy before rushing in to see Cathy. But though she wished that Marius Lyon's second sight of her had not found her in a nautical navy suit whose swinging skirt was short above long, shapely legs, and whose white sweater closely hugged full breasts, she knew that hindsight would not change what had happened.

Running a comb through her long thick hair she heard it crackle with electricity: a sure sign that she was still nervous. As always when she was in this mood the silver streak glowed brighter, and she combed it away from her forehead so that silver strands mingled with the chestnut brown, giving her hair a streaky blonde appearance that was the current fashion.

Hands buried in the pockets of her jacket, she went through the swing doors and turned towards Gower Street in search of a taxi. A dark green Rolls-Royce parked some few yards up the road glided in her direction, and as it came abreast of her a darkened window slid down and Marius Lyon's tanned face came into sight. Seen out of doors without the softening of electric light, his skin looked more bronze, which in turn made his hair appear greyer. It was strange they should both be prematurely grey, she thought, and wondered if his hair had always been this colour.

"I've been waiting for you," he said abruptly.

"I didn't realise you were." She did not slow her pace and the car spurted slightly to keep up with her, the chauffeur at the wheel staring impassively straight ahead as he did so.

"I didn't want Cathy to know," Marius Lyon went on. "It might have worried her."

"I don't see why," Philippa retorted, walking even faster. "You can't do me any more harm. You've already fired me."

"I might have been too precipitate about that." He opened the car door. "Get in."

"I've got to get back to the office."

"I'll drive you. Get in."

Deciding it was undignified to argue, she obeyed him. Going to close the door, her fingers fumbled on the handle and the door slipped open again, so that he had to lean across and slam it shut for her. She felt the weight of his leg against hers and saw his profile – the firm, large nose, the thick eyebrows and heavy-lidded eyes – before he settled back in the seat and the chauffeur set the limousine in motion again.

In the close confines of the car he seemed even bigger than he had in the hospital room. With his sheer size alone probably frightened his competitors to death! Her mouth twitched at the idea and she hastily lowered her eyes. They came to rest on the spatulate nails of one large hand. It was a beautifully shaped one, she noticed, with unusually long fingers.

"Your job's still available." The brusque words startled her. "Mrs. Hibberd would like you to take over the 'Dear Jessie' page."

"I'm working for *The Monitor*."

"Your salary would be considerably more," he went on as if she had not spoken. "I'm offering you your job back, Miss – er – "

"Rogers," Philippa said coldly, "and you're wasting your time, Mr. Lyon. I have no intention of working for you again."

"If you'd like me to apologise for what I said to you in my office, then please take it as done."

"It doesn't matter any more," she shrugged. "Anyway, I'd rather you didn't lie."

His glance was sharp. "Do you always have such a biting tongue?"

"When I have something to bite on."

He grunted, and she could not tell if the sound was one of amusement or anger. "I assume Cathy is using you as a relay station between herself and Alan Bedford," he remarked.

The statement caught Philippa off guard, and for the second time that day she was furious at her lack of perception. She should have guessed that a man of Marius Lyon's experience would know how Cathy's naïve intelligence would work.

"Don't deny it," he went on in the same even tones.

"I wasn't going to. If you'll tell me what else you want to know, I'll save you the trouble of further inspired guesses." Again she knew she had provoked him, for he half-slewed round and stared at her, his eyes so dark a grey without the light on them that they appeared almost black.

"Well, tell me," he said, in the quietest voice she had yet heard him use.

She slid further back into the corner. "I saw Alan Bedford for the first time last night. Cathy wanted me to tell him she still loved him, and to know if he – if he still loved her."

"Naturally he does – and will go on loving her to his dying day! Am I right?"

"He didn't put it quite like that," she said icily. "But he *is* still in love with her."

"I'll bet he is. She's a damn good meal-ticket for any man."

"Don't you think someone can love her for herself?"

"Some man will – but not yet. And not Bedford. She's too childish for him."

"That's *your* opinion."

"That's all I'm interested in!" His hand moved and she drew back so sharply that he stopped and stared at her. A gleam came into his eyes and his hand moved again, going to his breast pocket to take out a crocodile case and a cigar.

"I don't hit the women in my life," he said in conversational tones. "I have other means of bringing them to heel."

"I'm not one of your women!"

Ignoring her remark, he put a match to his cigar. "About Bedford," he said. "I don't suppose you'd listen if I asked you not to act as a go-between?"

"Not unless you gave me a good reason – other than your own irrational objection."

"You don't know what my objection is."

"He isn't rich."

At this she saw his temper rise. It was apparent in the flaring of his nostrils and the sudden narrowing of his lids. "I was poor myself once. Bedford's position is the last thing in the world I care about."

"Then why don't you like him?"

"Because he wouldn't look at Cathy if *she* were poor!"

"How do you know?"

"I've made it my business to find out about him."

"You mean you spied on him!"

"I looked into his background," Marius Lyon said calmly. "And what I have learned doesn't inspire me to any confidence. Don't be taken in by his Peter Pan appearance. He could give Casanova a good run for his money!"

"So could you." The words were out before she could stop them, and she was mortified with herself.

But he took them in his stride and merely shrugged. "I never promise marriage, Miss Rogers. And the women that I know are well able to take care of themselves."

"But Alan wants to *marry* Cathy."

"Only because she's my niece. The type of girl he likes is a well-stacked blonde who's good in bed! He was even living with one when he met Cathy."

"So what? If he was *still* living with her then – "

"He's too clever for that. The minute he learned who Cathy was he turfed out the girl-friend and – "

"That still doesn't show he doesn't love Cathy. Would *your* past prevent you from falling genuinely in love with someone in the future?"

"We're not talking about my love life."

"What's so special about it?" she said angrily. "You're sufficiently experienced to know that a man often marries a girl who's quite different from the ones he goes to bed with!"

"You're deliberately misunderstanding me. I tell you Cathy isn't his type."

"Are all your women the same type?"

"You could say that."

Curiosity stirred in her, but she quelled it instantly. "Even if you're right about Alan, you won't get Cathy to see it by going about it the way you are. The more you prevent her from seeing him the more she'll fight you."

"I didn't stop her from seeing him in the beginning. It was only when I saw she was serious that I objected."

"You shouldn't have done."

"Should I have waited for it to wear itself out? And if it didn't?"

"You'd be no worse off than you are now."

"What are you suggesting I do?"

She had not expected the question and the way he was leaning towards her – half angrily, half menacingly – told her it was not a rhetorical one.

"Let Cathy and Alan meet," she said hesitantly. "She can't walk, so you needn't be afraid of their eloping again."

The man's face grew bleak. "You hit hard."

"I didn't mean to in this instance. I was just trying to make you see they're not likely to run away at the moment. But if you prevent them meeting, Cathy will either use me or someone else to get messages to him. By making the whole affair clandestine you're only increasing its excitement. If you genuinely believe Alan is wrong for Cathy, or that she's only infatuated with him, give her the chance of getting to know him. If you're right, she'll fall out of love, and if you're wrong. . . ." Philippa squared her shoulders and then said bravely: "Perhaps you'll be honest enough to admit it and give them your blessing."

He was silent for so long that they travelled the length of Fleet Street without a word. Only as the car drew to a stop outside the brash portals of *The Monitor* did he come out of his reverie. "I'll let my niece meet Alan providing you promise to be there on each occasion."

"You must be joking! You can't make me Cathy's keeper."

"Those are my terms. If you want her happiness – "

"Don't you?"

"Of course I do. But I believe I can achieve it by keeping Alan out of her life. You believe the opposite. Neither of us will know who is right unless we give them a chance to meet."

"And if you found they did genuinely love each other?"

"Then they can marry – if and when Cathy can walk again."

The words were slow to impinge on Philippa's mind, but when they did they filled her with dread. "Are you saying that she – she might never walk again?"

"The doctors don't know for sure." Marius Lyon looked at the tip of his cigar. "I am telling you this in confidence. It is not to be repeated."

"Of course not." She blinked quickly to stop the sudden rush of tears that threatened to spill over. "But why must *I* be there when they meet? Surely I'm the last person you can trust!"

"On the contrary. You have already told Cathy to elope – with the disastrous results which you can see for yourself. You're hardly likely to encourage her to do it again!"

The words stabbed at her like a knife in a wound. "And you accuse me of hitting hard," she said jerkily.

"I only do what I have to do." He stepped out on to the pavement and waited for her to follow. "Do you agree to my terms?" he said again.

"You've made it impossible for me to refuse, haven't you?" she said quietly. "Do you always get your own way?"

"Yes," he said. "I do. I advise you to remember that for the future."

CHAPTER SEVEN

With Marius Lyon back in England, Philippa was careful to ensure he was not at the hospital when she went to see Cathy. It meant telephoning before each of her visits, but this slight embarrassment was better than the greater one of having to face him.

She had seen him once more since their extraordinary conversation in his car, but it had been for a fleeting moment only, when she had been leaving the hospital and he had been arriving in company with one of the doctors.

"Beats me why you're afraid of him," Cathy grumbled when Philippa, popping in to see her for a few moments on her way home from the office, looked anxiously at her watch. "He was here this morning, so he's not likely to come back again. Now I'm not at death's door he never comes more than once a day."

"I'm surprised he comes as often as that. If you were as rude to me as you are to him, I wouldn't come at all!"

"Don't tell me you're sticking up for him?" Cathy looked unexpectedly mischievous.

"I don't regard myself as your uncle's enemy," Philippa said stiffly. "I think he's very dictatorial, but he does have your best interests at heart."

"Don't you mean that he always thinks he knows what's best for everybody else?"

"I suppose so," Philippa smiled. "That makes him difficult to get on with, but it doesn't make him – " She hesitated, determined to be fair to him. "It doesn't make him unlovable."

Cathy gave a snort. "How lovable do *you* find him?"

"I wasn't talking personally."

"Then don't talk at all," came the rude reply. "I'm sick of generalisations."

Philippa stood up and immediately Cathy's face crumpled. "Please don't go, I didn't mean to be rude."

74

"Of course you did. You're a spoilt child and you need spanking."

"You can't hit a cripple," Cathy retorted bitterly.

At once Philippa's anger deserted her. Cathy could be rude, autocratic, and at times impossibly difficult to get on with, but one had to remember that she was frequently in pain and must be aware – though she was hiding it – of the possibility that she might never walk again. They were hardly circumstances to bring out the best in anyone, let alone a tempestuous and immature girl of eighteen.

"You really should try and control your temper," she chided. "I know it's hard for you at the moment, but – "

"I've always had a temper," Cathy said candidly. "Daddy had his head in the clouds and getting into a tantrum was the only way of making him notice me."

Pity tugged at Philippa. "Was he always busy with his work?"

"His work and his hobbies. He was a keen naturalist and a wonderful painter. He did some fantastic studies of moths. He never really knew what was going on around him," Cathy went on. "I'm sure he married Celia because she arranged it all."

As always when Cathy's stepmother was mentioned, Philippa tried to envisage her. But she could form no satisfactory image of her. A woman who had been happy to marry an unworldly civil servant-cum-naturalist did not fit in with the picture of an avaricious schemer intent on capturing her wealthy brother-in-law.

"What's bothering you?" Cathy asked.

"Your stepmother. If she was happily married to your father, then she isn't the type to have her eye on the main chance. And I certainly can't see her preventing you from marrying simply because she was afraid your uncle would send her away afterwards."

"I can't help whether you believe it or not," Cathy said stubbornly. "It happens to be true. Celia was only married to my father for a couple of months, you know. And marriage to Daddy – even though he was unworldly – gave her a better life than she had been living. I mean she had servants and a nice

75

house and a husband who was quite important. Before that, she was just a repressed spinster living on a fixed income."

"Miaow!" Philippa murmured.

Cathy smiled but refused to be deflected. "Celia has blossomed into her own since she's been living with Marius, and she has got no intention of moving out. Once she's got him to propose she wouldn't care if I eloped with a gorilla! But until she's made sure of her position she intends keeping me tied to her. As long as I'm single and living in my uncle's home, it's her home too."

It was the second time Philippa had heard this story, and though it might be true she had no means of checking it.

"You'll be seeing Celia for yourself," Cathy went on, divining her thoughts. "I should be home by the end of next week."

"Sooner than that," a gruff voice said from the doorway, and Philippa slewed round to see the man she was trying to avoid.

She jumped up so quickly that her chair toppled and would have fallen, had he not stepped forward and caught it. But beyond a cursory glance in her direction he paid her no attention, focusing it completely on his niece.

"That's why I came back to see you," he continued. "I saw Angus this afternoon and he says there's no reason why we can't take you home tomorrow, so long as we continue your physiotherapy every day."

"Are you sure I'll be able to manage by myself?" Cathy's face was unexpectedly pinched. "Everything's much easier here. The nurses know what I want and – "

"There'll be a nurse for you at home too," he interrupted roughly. "And your wheelchair will just fit into the lift, so there won't be any problem in getting to your bedroom."

Watching him, Philippa knew that his gruff tones were a mask for his feelings, for there was no mistaking the tender way he was patting his niece's arm. At the moment he was more like a great big grizzly bear than a lion, she thought inconsequentially and, unwilling to be in the way, she picked up her coat and inched to the door.

"Wait." There was no gruffness in Marius Lyon's voice as

he called to her, only a command that had to be obeyed. "I'll drive you home."

"I'm not going home," she lied.

"I want to talk to you, even so."

Reluctant to openly defy him, yet irritated at having to do as he ordered, she remained waiting by the door as he made arrangements to collect Cathy from the hospital the following day.

"There's no need for you to waste your valuable time picking me up," Cathy said with a return to her former rudeness. "Just send the chauffeur for me."

"Time spent on you is never wasted," her uncle replied with unexpected humour. "Learning to control my temper with you is good for my soul!"

Philippa smothered a laugh by turning it into a cough; the last thing she wanted was to let Cathy think she was on Marius Lyon's side, though watching the way he coped with the girl she knew an irresistible longing to give her a good shake. Had he always behaved in such a controlled and conciliatory fashion towards his niece, or did he too feel guilty for what had happened to her?

"I'll collect you in the morning, Cathy," he said, his voice loud in the small room. "I've ordered a special wheelchair for you and someone will be bringing it here to show you how to use it."

"What's special about it?" Cathy asked carelessly.

"It's motorised and has lots of gadgets. I brought it back with me from the States."

"Cheaper than a diamond bracelet for you. Isn't that the way you usually buy off the women in your life?"

For an instant he was silent, though his fresh complexion grew ruddy. "Count yourself lucky you're not one of my women," he said with quiet savagery, "or I'd make you very sorry for a remark like that."

Cathy's colour matched his, and watching them both, Philippa was struck by the similarity of spirit between them. Yet the man was bound to win in any battle. He was so strong and

77

commanding that no one – least of all a woman – could stand up to him.

"Somebody once gave me a game 'Happy Families'," Philippa said, breaking the tense silence. "And watching you both I suddenly remembered it!"

Cathy gave a gulp of laughter. "We are a happy family, aren't we, Marius? Locked together in hatred! Don't you think our relationship would make a good story for your readers? Wicked uncle controls life of invalid niece!"

"One day you'll be able to control your own life."

"How can I live a life in a wheelchair?"

"You'll walk again," he said quietly. "But in the meantime – "

"In the meantime I'll die of boredom," Cathy interrupted.

"In the meantime you can see Alan once a week."

Ready with another sarcastic retort, Cathy was astounded into silence. For several seconds she stared at her uncle, then seeing from his expression that he was not joking, she leaned forward. "You're really going to let me see Alan?"

"Yes. So long as Miss Rogers is with you each time."

"What's Philippa got to do with it?"

"I want her to be present when you see him. That is my only stipulation."

"What a crazy idea! Why can't I see him alone?"

He hesitated. "I don't wish to discuss it any more. I've told you my terms. You can take it or leave it."

"I'm old enough to do as I like," Cathy retorted. "And I won't be treated like an imbecile."

"You're an invalid," her uncle said harshly, "and you're totally dependent on me. I advise you to remember that!"

"What a hateful thing to say!" Cathy burst into noisy sobs, and with an exclamation Marius Lyon moved away from the bed.

For fully a minute he remained silent, watching his niece, then with a sigh he went to the door. "I'll wait for you in the corridor," he said quietly to Philippa. "I'll leave you to get her to see sense."

The door closed behind him and immediately Philippa ran to the bed and gathered Cathy close, feeling far more than only three years her senior. Most families had problems of one sort or another, but none were so noisy and difficult about them as these self-willed and obstinate Lyons.

"Do stop crying," she said finally, when Cathy still gave no sign of gaining control of herself. "You're being awfully stupid about the whole thing. If you had any sense you'd be crying for joy instead of temper."

"What have I got to be joyful about?"

"Because your uncle's letting you see Alan. Don't you realise it's his first step towards a climb-down?"

"That's what you think! He's just letting me see him because he knows I'll make myself ill if I don't."

"That isn't true," Philippa replied.

"Then why does he insist on *you* being there?"

"Because he isn't the sort of man who can bear to give in completely. He has to do it step by step." Philippa took a deep breath and as casually as she could, recounted some of the scene that had taken place between herself and Marius Lyon the week before. "So you see," she concluded, "you have misjudged him. If you can convince him that you and Alan are genuinely in love, he'll let you get married – when you're well again," she added quickly. "He only wants me to be with you to make sure you don't do anything foolish while you're still an invalid."

Several varying expressions passed over Cathy's face before she finally spoke. "So you're to be my watchdog? I suppose it could have been worse."

"It certainly could," Philippa said drily. "At least I'm house-trained and I don't bite!"

With the lightning change of mood which Philippa had grown to expect from her, Cathy burst out laughing. "Fancy Marius letting me see Alan. I'm sure it's all your doing. Did you make him realise how wrong he'd been?"

"Your uncle doesn't believe he's been wrong. He's merely willing to admit he may not always be right!"

"That's too fine a distinction for me to understand," Cathy grinned, and caught hold of Philippa's hand. "Do you think I

79

can call Alan and tell him the news, or are my calls still being monitored?"

"Monitored?" Philippa echoed.

"Don't look so surprised. I'm only allowed to make outgoing calls to the people Marius approves of. And Alan's not on the list."

"Maybe your uncle has reinstated him." Philippa was careful to keep her disquiet at Marius Lyon's behaviour out of her voice. Her aim was to cool the tension between him and Cathy, and to show her dislike of his high-handed action would have the opposite effect. "See if you can get through to him now," she suggested, and watched as Cathy picked up the telephone and gave Alan's number.

The telephonist promised to call back and Cathy put down the receiver and looked at Philippa with cynical eyes. One minute passed, and then another.

Cathy sighed. "It doesn't look as if – " The bell shrilled and she caught up the receiver, her face creasing into a radiant smile as she heard the voice at the other end.

"Alan darling," she burbled, "it's me – Cathy. Something wonderful has happened. Marius is going to let me see you again! We can't be on our own, but . . ."

Not waiting to hear any more, Philippa tiptoed out. She was at the lift door before she became aware of someone watching her, and looking round she saw Marius Lyon's broad-shouldered figure coming towards her.

"I told you I would wait for you," he said, sensing her surprise. "I want to talk to you."

"What about? You've got your own way."

"I always get it. I warned you of that." He motioned her to precede him into the lift and they went down to the ground floor. "If you'll tell me where you're going," he said as they reached the pavement, "I'll drive you there."

"Home," she replied.

"I thought you were going out."

"I lied. I said the first thing that came into my head."

"You're honest, at least."

"I always try to be."

"I'll remember that." He held the door open for her, and ungraciously she got into the front seat and watched as he closed the door and came round to take the driving wheel. He had a different car tonight: small and dark, with a throaty engine that growled ominously as it sprang into life.

"It's like riding on a tiger," she commented, as they shot smoothly out into the mainstream of traffic.

"I like a car with a lot of power."

"I've never seen one like this before."

"It's a custom-built Porsche." He shot her a swift look. "Do I detect a note of disapproval on your face?"

"Not at all. If you want to waste your money on toys like this . . ."

Unexpectedly he laughed, a deep sound that was full of humour. "I enjoy talking to you, Miss Rogers. You always say the unexpected."

"And the unwelcome."

"That too," he agreed. "But at least it makes for interest. There's nothing more boring than always knowing what someone is going to say. That happens too often in my life."

"It must be expensive for you."

"I beg your pardon?"

"The diamond bracelets," she reminded him.

He was silent for a moment as he crossed a busy intersection. "You shouldn't believe everything Cathy says about me."

"I don't have to listen to Cathy," Philippa said sweetly. "There are stacks of files on you in the reference library."

"Do they list the bracelets?"

"Only the names of your many ex-friends."

"Are you trying to make me feel embarrassed, Miss Rogers?"

"I'd never try anything that was doomed to failure."

Again his laugh came. "Let's talk about you for a change. Is your past worth delving into?"

"I doubt it. It's very innocuous."

"The only girl in a family of two brothers. Doting parents who gave you an excellent schooling and now have the intelligence to let you live your own life."

"If that's an inspired guess," she said breathlessly.

"A fifty pounds guess," he cut across her. "It cost me that to get a good inquiry agent."

"A what?"

"A detective agency. I thought that was better than getting one of my reporters to look into your background. I prefer to keep my private affairs out of my business."

"I never knew I was your private affair," she said icily.

"You're involved with my niece. It was important I check up on you."

"Can't you form your own assessment without relying on snoopers?"

"I didn't think it right to rely on my own judgment. Our meetings so far have not allowed me to form an unbiased judgment of you."

"I assume I've now passed the test?"

"With flying colours."

She knew an irrational longing to swing round and hit him, but glancing at his huge bulk she realised the futility of doing so. So must David have felt when faced with Goliath. Yet David had felled the giant. . . . She sighed, and wondered what was the modern equivalent of a sling and arrow.

"You had no right to tell Cathy I had agreed to act as a chaperone," she said in the silence. "I hadn't finally made up my mind about it."

"That was why I made it up for you!"

She caught her breath. "You're the most obnoxious man I know!"

"I don't disagree with you, Miss Rogers, but I'm more concerned with Cathy's welfare than your opinion of me."

"I'm concerned with her welfare, too."

"Then you would eventually have agreed to do as I had asked."

"Yes, but – "

"Forget the buts and just leave it at the 'yes'." He slowed the car. "If you can tell me where you live. . . ."

She looked through the window, surprised to see they were in St. John's Wood. "You've come in the right direction."

"Your address was in the detective's report," he said, and pretended not to hear her exclamation. "You live in one of the blocks along here, I believe?"

"On the corner of the next turning," she said coldly, and remained aloof as he drew the car into the kerb, opened the door for her and escorted her to the entrance of the apartment house.

"We both have a moral responsibility towards Cathy," he said suddenly. "I feel as guilty about her as you do."

"I wish you'd let me cope with my guilt in my own way."

"Not as long as I need your help."

"I'll do everything I can for her, Mr. Lyon, but I won't have you bully me!"

"Then stop fighting me and do as I say," he said harshly. "Cathy has a long fight ahead of her if she is going to walk again. If I can be sure that Alan's the right man for her—"

"How can I help you find that out?"

"I respect your judgment."

"You didn't respect it when I told Cathy to elope."

The remark brought him up short and he frowned. "Let's not talk about the past. My concern is with the future. Just be at the house each week when Alan's there. At the end of three months we can pool our information and see where we get to."

"I'm damned if I'll spy for you!"

"You'll regret it if you don't."

"Are you threatening me?" she cried.

"Yes, I am. If you don't do as I ask, I'll get you fired from *The Monitor. And* I'll see you never get a job in Fleet Street again!"

"You wouldn't dare!" She stared at him in fury, her conviction dying as she saw the expression in his eyes. Oh yes, he would. He certainly would. "I don't merely dislike you, Mr. Lyon," she said icily. "I despise you."

His laugh, hard and unamused, followed her as she swung on her heel and went into the lobby. As she turned to go up in

83

the lift she saw him still standing on the steps, a tall dark shadow; but unlike a shadow, she knew he would not disappear from her life in the daylight.

CHAPTER EIGHT

For a week after her meeting with Marius Lyon, Philippa did not go and see Cathy. The man's blunt assertion that he could command her to do as he wanted had left her raw with anger, and she wished she had the courage to call his bluff. Surely he would never dare get her fired from her job, nor try to prevent her getting another one? If he did, he ran the risk of her complaining to the Union of Journalists and it could well result in a strike of his own staff. But before that happened she would have to prove his involvement, and this might be difficult, if not impossible. A few well-chosen words into the right ear and his actions would sink without trace, leaving no evidence for her to use against him.

Yet it was not the threat of being forced to leave Fleet Street which finally brought her to his elegant town house in Belgravia, but a call from Cathy, tearfully inquiring when she would be coming to see her.

"Alan wants to come round," she pleaded, "but Marius insists on your being here. Please come, Philippa. I'm so miserable."

Knowing herself beaten, Philippa went.

Marius Lyon's home surprised her. It was the end one in a row of large terraced houses, set to one side of a quiet, Embassy-dominated square. The white stone exterior was as discreet as the narrow windows and gave no indication of the beauty within: glittering chandeliers sparkling down on marble floors covered with glowing Persian rugs; silk and velvet draperies muting the hum of traffic and brocade-covered settees inviting one to rest and relax. The atmosphere of restfulness surprised her more than anything, for she had never considered the newspaper tycoon to be a man of tranquillity. But there was no denying that his home exuded this; and not only tranquillity but culture too. It was apparent in the pictures that lined the walls: most of them fabulously expensive but a surprising number being subtle watercolours and delicate etchings, and the vast array of books stacked not only on shelves but overflowing on to tables, and giving an atmosphere of casual living to what might otherwise have looked like an interior decorator's opulent dream.

"Has your uncle lived here long?" she asked Cathy, unable to hide her curiosity.

"Ever since I can remember. I know my father always wrote to him at this address." Cathy looked around her. "It's a nice place, isn't it? My uncle has good taste."

"You mean he furnished it himself?"

"Can you see him leaving it to anyone else?" came the amused comment. "I bet he even chose the saucepans in the kitchen!"

Not waiting for a reply, Cathy deftly swung her wheelchair into the drawing-room. The week away from the hospital had helped to restore the colour to her cheeks, though there was still a noticeable tenseness in her voice and movements.

"Alan should be arriving any minute." Her words explained her tautness. "Do you know it's the first time I've seen him for six weeks? I'm so excited, I feel ill."

"You look fine," Philippa assured her. "You're positively glowing."

"That's my make-up," Cathy blinked her false eyelashes. "Do you like it?"

Philippa nodded, unwilling to lie openly. The heavy foundation and brightly painted lids made Cathy look like a little girl who had been dabbling too heavily into pots of paint. But it made her look pathetic too, and she hoped this was what Alan would notice, rather than the sticky look of the over-rouged mouth and the mascaraed black lashes which were reminiscent of a vampire.

An elderly butler wheeled in a trolley and silently set it by the fireplace. Upon a silver tray stood with a graceful Georgian tea-set and translucent white and gold china, though there was nothing dainty about the large plate of warm crumpets bubbling with butter that nestled in a silver-covered dish.

"Alan's coming straight from work," Cathy explained. "And he'll be starving."

"Wouldn't it have been better if you had invited him to dinner?"

"He's going back to work. He's doing a lot of overtime so that he can earn extra money."

Involuntarily Philippa's eyes went to the Renoir above the mantelpiece. Trapped forever on canvas were the pink and white charms of a plump young woman fondling a pink and white child, both sitting on an emerald-green lawn beneath an electric blue sky. The painting alone was worth more than Alan was likely to earn in ten years, and it made Cathy's remark seem ridiculous. Philippa bit her lip. She was forgetting that Marius Lyon was only Cathy's uncle, and though he might love her, it was not with the same depth of feeling as a father. What would my own father do if I suddenly told him I wanted to marry a penniless young man? she wondered. Would he also suspect the love of being mercenary or would he be willing to rely on my judgment and do everything he could to help me? Certainly if he was satisfied about the man's love he would never allow him to struggle for a living while an expensive painting hung on his mantelshelf. But Marius Lyon seemed to believe that one must work for what one got, and not look to anyone else for help. She sighed and wondered if he felt like this because no one had helped him when he himself had been struggling for success. She must look at his press cuttings again in the reference library. It would be interesting to read up on his early beginnings.

A knock at the door heralded Alan's arrival, and Philippa moved to the corner of the room and made herself as unobtrusive as possible as she heard Cathy's broken exclamations of pleasure and saw Alan's warm gesture of love as he knelt by the wheelchair.

It was several moments before either of them realised she was half hiding behind a curtain, and then Alan came across to her, casual in black slacks and sweater, and looking more like a ballet dancer than a mechanic. But his hands, as they gripped hers, were surprisingly strong, the skin hard and rough.

"Hello, Phil. So you're our miracle worker, eh? Are you our clock-watcher too?"

"If I am, I haven't been told about it."

"Good. I was afraid you'd turn me into a toad if I didn't leave on the hour!"

"You're more likely to turn into a racing car," Cathy grinned. "Then you could go racing off somewhere else!"

"You've put an end to my racing days," he grinned as he returned to the settee beside her. "I'm not going to Brands Hatch till you can come with me."

"That might not be for months. Even longer."

"Rubbish! I've no intention of leaving my wife at home all the time – even if she *is* stuck in a wheelchair."

Cathy's cheeks flamed. "What – what do you mean?"

"That I intend to marry you as soon as I can get your uncle to say yes."

"He'd never do that while I can't walk."

"I'm not suggesting we ask him tomorrow," Alan replied. "I was thinking of a couple of months' time when he's realised that the quickest way of giving you back your health is to let you marry me."

"Do you really think he might?" Cathy asked excitedly.

"Sure I do. That's why he's caved in and let me come here." He glanced round the room appraisingly. "He looks after you better than I could."

"I'd be happy in two rooms as long as I was sharing them with you."

"I want more than two rooms for you." He caught Cathy's hand that lay on the blankets covering her legs. "You're my special girl and I want to give you the world."

Philippa felt more intrusive than at any time in her life, and with a faint murmur she retreated from the room. Marius Lyon had insisted she be in the house each time Alan saw Cathy, but he had not stipulated that she had to remain with them, and she intended to take full advantage of the loophole.

Time passed slowly as she remained in the hall. She knew there were other rooms in which she could sit, but was unwilling to go exploring. Restlessly she walked to the front door and peered through one of the narrow windows beside it. It was dark outside and a street lamp glowed on pavements wet with rain. She could discern the lights of many cars crossing the square, but double glazing cut off most of the sound and it was like looking at a television screen with the volume turned down.

Suddenly she became aware that she was not alone. A delicate perfume made her nostrils twitch and she turned and saw she was being watched by a woman as subtle in looks and dress as the scent that drifted around her as she came close.

Without being told, Philippa knew it was Celia Lyon. Not that the woman was in any way as she had imagined. She was so pale a blonde as to be almost silver, the fine-spun hair drawn back into an old-fashioned loop on the nape of her neck. The style gave dignity to her rather square face and lent refinement to the small, full mouth and the short nose which was slightly too thick to be called classical. Her best feature was her eyes, large and serene and so pale a grey they seemed more like mirrors, able to reflect the colours around her. Now they reflected the green of Philippa's dress and gave the woman a cat-like quality, an illusion heightened by the thick lids which came slowly down over the irises, as though masking the thoughts that lay behind them.

"You must be Philippa," she said, and her voice was like a cat too, but a contented cat who had drunk the cream.

Philippa nodded. "You are Cathy's stepmother."

"Yes, I am. But why are you in the hall? I thought I heard Alan arrive?"

"He's in the drawing-room with Cathy. There didn't seem any harm in leaving them alone for a while."

The woman shrugged, and turning, opened the door of a small sitting-room. "You'll find it more comfortable to wait in here."

"What a lovely room," Philippa remarked, as she saw the Wedgwood blue carpet and the exquisite Chinese porcelain that stood in skilfully lighted cabinets.

"It's my brother-in-law's favourite. He always comes in here to relax when he's had a difficult day." She made a gesture for Philippa to sit down, and then stood in front of her, her expression curious.

"You're older than I thought, Miss Rogers. Marius gave me the impression you were Cathy's age. He said you were a child." Sharp little teeth bit on the full lower lip in a gesture of embarrassment that Philippa knew was false.

"I'm twenty-one," she said composedly. "That's hardly a child these days."

"It depends on one's character, I think. Cathy will be a baby no matter how old she is."

Unwilling to comment on this, Philippa said nothing, and Celia Lyon went over to a chair. She was the same height as Philippa but bone-thin, with slender ankles and arms, though her hands were surprisingly large and bony. They were her ugliest feature, Philippa decided, and knew the woman thought so too, for as she sat down she hid them beneath the folds of her grey chiffon dress. Only someone with supreme fashion sense would have worn such a subdued colour, for its muted shade gave depth to the blue-white skin and lustre to the pale hair.

Beside such soignée chic, Philippa felt her own chestnut hair and full-breasted figure to be over-stated: a ridiculous idea, she thought, and dismissed it at once.

"I believe you used to work for my brother-in-law," the woman said.

"Yes. But the only time I saw him was when he fired me!"

Celia Lyon laughed. It was her first spontaneous action and it made her look surprisingly pretty. "He *can* be rather aloof, I'm afraid. It's really because basically he's shy. Big men often are."

The mawkish sentimentality of the remark irritated Philippa. If the newspaper tycoon was shy, then pigs would be flying tomorrow! Deciding she did not relish being taken for a fool, she stood up.

"I'd better go back to Cathy," she murmured.

"There's no need to rush away. Stay and tell me what you think of my stepdaughter."

Faintly repelled at being expected to talk about someone she regarded as a friend, Philippa said stiffly: "I like her very much."

"You don't know her as well as I do. She can be exceedingly trying."

"She's still far from well."

"She's always been difficult. It's not to be wondered at really, when one thinks of the way she was brought up. Her parents were so unworldly."

"It must have been difficult for you to have been left with a stepdaughter so soon after you were married," Philippa said for want of something to say.

"It wasn't easy," the woman conceded. "But Marius has been wonderful."

Big men often are, Philippa thought to herself, and bit her lip to stop it from curving into a smile.

As though sensing Philippa's amusement, Celia Lyon shot her a suspicious look. "Cathy and I were left penniless, except for a small pension."

"Poverty is relative," Philippa commented.

"A wealthy relative as far as I'm concerned." The woman laughed at her own joke. "Marius couldn't be more generous to us. It's wonderful to find someone with such a strong sense of family."

"Too strong, I think," Philippa blurted out.

"Because he doesn't want Cathy to marry Alan? My dear girl, I agree with him."

"I know Alan's poor, but –"

"And Cathy's too young. That's the main reason. And please don't tell me again that she's eighteen. In experience she's a child."

Once more Philippa held her peace. She was wary of this woman who – though she looked like a placid china doll – had a shellac quality about her that made her calm exterior seem false. Annoyed with herself for being fanciful, and putting it down to pangs of hunger – it was a long time since her meagre lunch of coffee and ham roll – she tried to smother her antagonism.

"You may be right about Cathy being young for her age,"

she said calmly, "but at least Mr. Lyon has agreed to let her see Alan. Perhaps it will give you both a chance to revise your opinion of him."

"We're hoping Cathy will revise *hers*."

Remembering the scene that had recently taken place in the drawing room, Philippa doubted this. The very lack of sentimentality with which Alan had spoken of his future with Cathy had impressed her far more than any passionate outburst would have done. But it was unwise to say so, and she stared diplomatically down at the carpet.

Unexpectedly the centre light sprang into life: a magnificent affair of hand-painted china and glass, it illuminated the large figure of the man who stood on the threshold. What an aptitude Marius Lyon had for arriving when he was least expected, Philippa thought, and watched as he came forward.

He dwarfed the room with his size, yet he moved with the quietness of a panther. But it was a tired panther tonight: one who had fought hard and was drained of energy. He sank heavily into an armchair and without a word Celia went over to a satinwood sideboard and poured out a glass of whisky. Still in silence she gave it to him and he drained it at a gulp. Then he rested his head on the chair, his eyes closed, body relaxing completely.

Celia took the glass from his hand and, placing it back on the tray, quietly resumed her seat. She kept her eyes fixed on his face, but he seemed unaware of being watched, uncaring too, Philippa decided, for he was so arrogantly sure of his own importance. Not that he looked particularly important at this moment, she had to admit; just a tired man drained of vitality. Except for his hair. That glowed with a life of its own, springing back from his forehead in a silver-grey mane.

With his eyes closed she was aware of the lines on his face, the deep one that ran horizontally across his forehead, the fine network on his lids and the two heavy ones that ran down either side of his nose to his mouth. In repose his mouth was different too, the lower lip fuller and the upper one less thin and hard. With a suddenness that startled her his eyes opened and stared directly into hers, their grey depths kindling as they took in her expression. But he did not speak and merely raised his shoulders and stretched himself.

"That's better," he said, his voice vibrant again.

"I don't know how you do it, Marius," said Celia. "I've heard of catnaps, but yours are ridiculous. Two minutes of unconsciousness and you're completely recharged!"

He smiled. "I've a unique metabolism."

"You'd better not let your enemies have the secret."

"Enemies can't harm me now."

"Can one ever be that secure?" Philippa could not help asking.

He looked at her with faint surprise, but took a moment before he answered. "From enemies, yes. One reaches a state of success that makes it almost impossible for them to touch you. But there are others from whom one is never immune."

"Others?"

"People you love," he said, and abruptly changed the subject to ask his sister-in-law where Cathy was.

"She's with Alan, in the drawing-room."

With an oath he sat up straight and glared at Philippa. "I thought I told you not to leave them alone!"

"I'm not their jailer," she flared. "Alan isn't going to *steal* Cathy. He merely wants to marry her!"

"Over my dead body!"

"Then why are you letting them meet? I thought you were keeping an open mind about him?"

"My mind's open all right," he growled. "It's yours that's closed! If it weren't, you'd see for yourself the sort of man he is. My one hope is that Cathy's enough of a Lyon to wake up to him before it's too late!"

Philippa bit back the urge to tell him how wrong he was. Judging by the look of him he was in no mood to listen to unpalatable facts. Indeed he looked so furious that he gave the impression of a wild animal controlled by a very tight leash. She shivered. Far be it for her to do anything that would cause the leash to snap.

"How long has he been here?" came the staccato question.

"About an hour. You didn't stipulate how long he could stay."

"I didn't mean twenty-four-hour visits either! Go in and break it up."

Resenting the peremptory tone, she went out. If only Cathy had not come to her that night six weeks ago, and if only she had not given her any advice. How happy her life had been before the tempestuous Lyon family had come into it.

She knocked at the drawing-room door and slowly turned the handle, giving Alan time to move away from Cathy; but when she went in she found him bent over the wheelchair, his arms around her shoulders. Without any embarrassment he straightened and she was again reminded of something faunlike about him. Perhaps it was the easy way he moved, or his colouring. Certainly he was the total opposite to the volatile girl beside him, and would probably be well able to control her because of it.

"Is my time up?" he asked equably.

"You don't have to clock in or out," she said with a slight smile. "As you're only seeing Cathy once a week, you don't need to rush away."

"I don't see why it's only once a week either," Cathy interrupted. "If Marius is going to let Alan see me, why can't he be decent about it and let us meet whenever we like?"

"You'd do better to take that up with your uncle."

"He won't talk about it. Once he makes up his mind, you can't budge him."

"Don't try," said Alan. "Personally, I consider it a miracle he's letting us meet at all."

"I'd be your wife if it hadn't been for that accident," Cathy said fiercely. "When I think of it. . . ." She looked ready to dissolve into tears, and Alan leaned over and kissed her cheek.

"We'll have our future yet. I promise you that." Pulling away from her clinging hands, he went to the door.

"I wish you didn't have to work overtime," she wailed.

"We'll need the extra cash when we get – " He stopped, but made no attempt to cover up what he had said.

There was something extraordinary about his attitude,

Philippa felt. It was as if he believed it was only a matter of time before he and Cathy were together. Perhaps it was his way of trying to pretend the accident had never happened, and that Cathy was not facing several years in a wheelchair, possibly even the rest of her life.

Crossing the hall with him to the front door, she told him what was in her mind, and was taken aback by his sharp reaction.

"Cathy won't be in a wheelchair for life, nor for two years either. Her uncle's trying to frighten you."

"Why should he do that?"

"Perhaps it's more accurate to say he's trying to frighten *me*. He's hoping he'll scare me off – hoping I won't want Cathy if she can't walk."

"Would you? You're a young man: what life would you have married to someone who couldn't walk?"

"Don't talk rot."

"I'm trying to make you see facts."

"Illusions, you mean." He looked amused. "Because Mr. Lyon says something, it doesn't mean it's a fact. Remember that, Phil, before you start quoting him to me, or don't you mind being brainwashed by him?"

She reddened. "No one's brainwashing me."

"Then close your ears when he starts talking!" Alan advised, and raised his hand in a gesture of farewell. "I'll see you next week, unless you can persuade the great dictator to let me come before then. Perhaps if you told him you thought I'd done Cathy some good – "

"I will – if I think you have," Philippa retorted, and heard him chuckle as he went down to the motor bike parked by the kerb, a few inches from Marius Lyon's gleaming Rolls.

What was the best thing she could do for Cathy's happiness and future? she asked herself as she closed the door and leaned her back on it. On the positive side she was sure that Cathy's meetings with Alan would help her psychologically, but she was also afraid that as her physical well-being improved, his proximity would make her restless. Yet this was a chance that had to be taken. Even though she could not walk, Cathy could still lead a normal physical life; Philippa's thoughts raced ahead, seeing pictures that filled her with vague disquiet. Despite what Alan had said, she did not think he realised the problems involved in marrying an invalid. Money would help, of course, and if Mr. Lyon were generous then many of Cathy's problems could be overcome. Was this what Alan was hoping for? She sighed. Her whole future seemed to be dominated by Cathy's bleak prospects and Marius Lyon's overwhelming personality. It was time she stopped thinking about them and went on with her own life. She was not going to allow an arrogant man to feed on her guilt and use her, either as his whipping-boy or his spy.

CHAPTER NINE

Philippa's hope of saying goodbye to Cathy and leaving was forestalled by learning she was expected to stay to dinner.

"How did you know I didn't have a date?" she asked.

"I took a chance on it," Cathy grinned. "Anyway, you could always have brought him here."

"Like a little dog on a lead?"

"Who is he?"

"Who is who?"

"Your date."

"I never said I had one. I merely wondered what would have happened if – "

"Oh, I see. I just thought you *might* have a boy-friend tucked away somewhere."

"I'm quite fancy free," Philippa said composedly. "And I've no desire to change my status."

"Wouldn't you like to get married?"

"If and when I fall in love."

"Have you ever been in love?"

"Not seriously."

"Have you had lots of affairs?"

"Hundreds," Philippa quipped, and then immediately shook her head as she saw that Cathy was looking at her with great seriousness. "Of course I haven't. What made you think I had?"

"Because most journalists seem so emancipated. And the things they write are – "

"Journalists write about other people," Philippa interrupted, "rarely about themselves. Most of us are too hard-working to lead the life you imagine we do!"

"You mean you've honestly had no affairs?"

"Honestly," Philippa said firmly. "Now stop the catechism and talk about something else."

Cathy did as she was told and for the next hour they chatted on a variety of subjects. The girl was unexpectedly well read, with an extremely good knowledge of current affairs, both social and political, and it was not difficult to guess that her interest and knowledge stemmed from her uncle, whose opinions, she frankly admitted, were less radical than her own.

"You should hear us when we get going on politics," she giggled. "In fact it would be difficult not to. The walls almost fall down!"

"Are your rows always noisy?"

"We don't row over politics – we just disagree. Loudly."

"I'm surprised your uncle bothers discussing them with you."

"He loves nothing better than to try and make people change their minds. That's why his papers are so good. They always take a stand for what they believe in."

"For what *he* believes in, you mean."

"What's wrong with that? He owns the papers and he's entitled to have them say what he wants."

"Some people think newspapers should only give facts."

"It's a rare fact that isn't biased in some way or another," Cathy said flatly. "And none of my uncle's papers pretend they're totally factual. They're committed to a policy and they stick to it."

Philippa diplomatically remained quiet. It was the first time she had heard Cathy defend her uncle and it made her realise how similar the man and girl were in temperament: yet in the man, years of hard work had knocked off the rough edges and smoothed the rugged personality into a semblance of urbanity, while Cathy was still rough-grained, her mind a confusion of too many different ideas which she had not yet been able to coherently assimilate. It was easy to appreciate why Marius Lyon wanted her to go to university. She would receive a training there that would stand her in good stead when the mantle of his power eventually fell upon her shoulders.

Philippa sat up straight, her meandering thoughts jerked back to the present by the realisation of where they had led her. Marius Lyon was still young enough to marry and have children of his own to inherit his vast empire. There was no reason to think it would be left to nis niece.

"I met your stepmother," she said aloud, and the words – coming out of their own volition – made her realise the strength of thought association. Freud had certainly known a thing or two! "She was charming to me."

"She's like a bowl of yoghurt," Cathy retorted. "She looks like cream, but when you taste it, it's thin and sharp!"

"I'm afraid I don't know her well enough to give an opinion," said Philippa.

"You mean you don't want to!" Cathy stirred restlessly in her chair. "Do you see her as my uncle's wife?"

"I can't see anyone as his wife," Philippa said truthfully. "It wouldn't be a very enviable role."

"I don't see why. Once he believed someone loved him for what he was and not for what he could give them, he'd be a super husband."

"Be careful what you say," Philippa warned, "or I might think you like him!"

"I did like him until he started laying down the law about Alan. I never believed he'd be so determined to get his own way."

"You're determined too."

"Only about *my* life: not anyone else's!"

The point was valid and Philippa conceded it. The more she talked to Cathy, the more sensible she discovered her to be. When a few years of experience had dredged away the naïvety, she could well become a young tycoon in her own right!

"Let's go to my room and get ready for dinner," Cathy said suddenly, and without waiting for a reply, wheeled her chair towards the small lift in the hall.

It glided silently past two floors and came to a stop at the third. Here too the house was beautifully furnished, and bedrooms, each with its own bathroom, led off the small corridor.

"Celia and I share this floor," Cathy said, as Philippa followed the wheelchair across the cinnamon brown carpet to a large bedroom overlooking the square, "and my uncle has the top one. It's got its own terrace on the roof and glass walls that come up when you press a button!"

"What for?"

"To keep off the cold breeze when he sunbathes in the nude!"

The words brought such a vivid picture of him to mind that Philippa's cheeks burned. Hastily she turned to the mirror on the dressing table and made a pretence of combing her hair.

"I like that white streak of yours," Cathy remarked. "It gives you a sun-blonde look."

Philippa went on combing her hair. Although she had hoped to avoid Marius Lyon when she came here tonight, she had nevertheless taken care with her appearance on the luckless chance that she might not be able to do so, and she was glad she had chosen a green suit and matching chiffon blouse which, when she removed the jacket, allowed the pink of her skin to glow through. A softly frilled collar framed her neck, and exceptionally full sleeves were gathered into a frill at her wrists. The severity of the pencil-slim skirt contrasted with the femininity of the blouse, its softness heightened by her long shining hair which swung heavily to her shoulders and rippled like brown velvet each time she moved. Gaining confidence from her appearance, she turned away from the mirror and found Cathy watching her.

"I never realised how stunning you were."

"I get suspicious when you start flattering me," Philippa said lightly. "You'd do better to save your compliments for your stepmother."

"She'd lap them up. She loves being told how wonderful she is. Not that she'd believe me if *I* said so. She knows I can't stand her!"

"Shall we go downstairs again?" Philippa suggested quickly, anxious to keep Cathy off a subject that would only upset her.

"What's the rush? Or don't you like me criticising my beloved stepmother? When you know her as well as I do, you'll dislike her too. Sometimes I think she only married my father in order to wriggle her way into Marius' life."

"Aren't you letting your prejudice run away with you?"

Philippa said tactfully. "After all, when she married your father she had no idea he was going to die so suddenly."

"She married him with the intention of making him come to England and take a job with Marius. That would have brought her right into my uncle's life."

"She would still have been your father's wife," Philippa insisted. "And I can't see your uncle doing anything to. . . . No, I'm sure you're wrong."

"I'm not." Cathy refused to be dissuaded. "I don't know what she intended doing about my father – probably have poisoned him to get him out of the way – but I'm certain she had her sights on Marius."

"Don't say things like that! Apart from it being libellous, it's horrible."

"Facts often are."

"Facts are coloured by people's prejudices," Philippa retorted. "You said so yourself. And you have to admit you're extremely prejudiced." Cathy's shrug did not disprove the point and Philippa pressed home her advantage. "Anyway, your uncle has a mind of his own and no one can force him to do anything he doesn't want to do. He has such a strong sense of family he'd never have done anything to hurt your father."

"I never said Marius *would*." Cathy was indignant. "I was only saying what Celia would have done. Anyway, things worked out just the way she wanted them. Daddy died within months of her marrying him and we were settled in here." The wheelchair spun forward to the centre of the room. "I thought she'd have got him before now. I mean, four years is a long time to stalk your prey!"

"What horrible metaphors you use!"

"They're very fitting."

Philippa did not demur, and though she knew it would have been discreet to let the conversation lapse, Cathy's remarks had roused her curiosity to a pitch where it had to be satisfied. Despite Marius Lyon's numerous love affairs, she felt him to be a man who would wish to perpetuate what his drive and talent had created. This meant producing sons who would inherit his empire, and this in turn meant a wife. Taking this to be true, surely the fair Celia could have won him by now? The fact that she had not done indicated his unwillingness to marry her.

Tentatively she said so to Cathy, who gnawed at the statement like a dog at a bone.

"For the first couple of years my uncle only saw Celia as Daddy's widow, and for him that made her untouchable. It's only in the past year that he's started thinking of her as a woman he could have." She frowned. "I don't think he's had her *yet*."

"I'm surprised you can't be more positive," Philippa said sarcastically. "I assumed you'd spied on them to find out!"

"I did from time to time, but I never saw anything."

Philippa could not help laughing. There was something so disarming about Cathy's frankness that it was difficult to be angry with her. "Let's go down and eat," she suggested, changing the subject. "I'm starving."

"The gong hasn't gone yet," said Cathy, and stopped as she heard one reverberate through the house. "There it is." She pressed a button on the side of her chair and the wheels moved. "Mush, mush!"

As they emerged from the lift to the ground floor, the man and woman they had been speaking about were framed in the doorway of the dining room, and only then did Philippa know for sure that she was not dining alone with Cathy. Her cheeks burned with embarrassment, for she felt herself to be in the way, and was certain the girl had deliberately engineered for her to stay without letting anyone know. But in this she was proved wrong, for as they entered the dining-room Marius Lyon indicated her to take the chair on his right, and said:

"Cathy chose the meal tonight in your honour, and it took all my influence to get it done in time."

Philippa's mystification died as she stared at the table. An assortment of small silver gilt bowls filled with a variety of different sauces showed they were dining Eastern style, a fact that was confirmed as the first course was set before her – sweet and sour shrimp soup, with tiny pieces of red chilli floating on its surface. Soup was followed by heaped bowls of boiled white rice, cooked without salt or seasoning so that its blandness could temper the highly-spiced dishes that accompanied it: morsels of chicken crisped in oil and smothered in garlic sauce, tidbits of pork spiked on pineapple cubes and the succulent white flesh of lobsters doused in hot peppers. It was the lobsters which told her what her host had meant about having to use his influence, for these were no erstwhile residents of cold Atlantic waters, but had come direct from the Bay of Siam, as indeed his next words indicated.

"Delivered to London Airport this morning by courtesy of B.O.A.C."

Embarrassment, as unexpected as it was unwanted, tied Philippa's tongue, and it was left to Celia to pick up the conversation.

"Do you have any special interest in Thailand, Miss Rogers?"

"Not really," she said reluctantly. "But I was supposed to – I was going for a holiday and it was cancelled."

"What Philippa means is that a whole group were going from the Features Section of *Today's News*," Cathy explained, "but her ticket was cancelled when Marius fired her."

"Cathy!" Philippa choked, but the younger girl looked unrepentant.

"That's why we're giving you a Thai dinner. Marius thought it was the very least he could do. Aren't I right?" she said directly to her uncle.

He nodded without speaking, and Philippa was not sure whether he was humouring his niece or actually agreeing with her. Not that she could imagine his regretting any of his actions. Hadn't he himself said that once he made up his mind he never changed it?

"I understand you're working for another paper," Celia said, continuing in her role of the gracious hostess.

"I'm with *The Monitor*."

"I think a girl must be awfully strong-minded to brave the rigours of Fleet Street. Journalism's such a hardboiled job."

"It's very rewarding."

"I'm sure the money's excellent, but –"

"I didn't mean money," Philippa interrupted. "I meant the actual work one does."

"What do *you* do?"

"At the moment I'm on Features. The editor hasn't finally decided where to put me."

Celia's obvious disappointment in the answer made Philippa aware of how dull her job must sound, and she cast a fleeting look at her host. But he appeared oblivious of the conversation, and she was certain he had closed his mind to it and was thinking of other more important things.

Celia was speaking again. "Tell me, Miss Rogers, are you one of our emancipated women who think a career is more important than marriage?"

"I don't like the words emancipated female," Philippa said bluntly. "That's very old-fashioned phraseology these days."

"I'm afraid I'm an old-fashioned person," came the reply. "I always disliked the idea of working in a job. I suppose it's because I'm a born homemaker."

"Some women do both!"

The entry of the butler to ask where they wished to take coffee put an end to a dialogue that was growing increasingly more explosive.

"No coffee for me," said Marius, seemingly returning to the present. "I have to go out. But serve it in the sitting-room." He looked at Cathy. "*You* must go to bed."

"I'm not tired."

"You're still going to bed. The physiotherapist said you should have plenty of rest."

"Can Philippa stay with me?"

"I'm going home," Philippa said quickly, anxious to prevent an argument.

"When will you come and see me again?"

"I'll phone you."

"I'll drive you home," said Marius Lyon, pushing back his chair.

"Please don't bother. I can easily get a taxi."

"Fetch your coat." Ignoring her remark, he moved across to

Celia who stood like a lonely dove in her pale grey chiffon. "I'm sorry I must leave you, my dear," his voice was astonishingly gentle, "but there's a strike at one of the other nationals and I promised to see if I could get the two sides together."

Celia's sadness lifted as though a magic wand had been waved over her, and Philippa knew without being told that the woman had been afraid she was being deserted for someone else.

"I'll wait up for you, Marius," she murmured.

"Don't do that. I might be very late."

"Then I'll have a hot drink and some sandwiches left in your room. You always get hungry after you've lost your temper!"

"What makes you so sure I'm going to lose my temper?" he chuckled.

Celia echoed his amusement, and walked with him into the hall, leaving Philippa to collect her jacket, say goodnight to Cathy and then go out to the waiting Rolls.

"There was no need for you to take me home," she said as they moved away from the kerb. "I could easily have got a taxi."

"I didn't know if you had an expense account on *The Monitor*!"

"I don't charge my private expenses."

"You're not like most journalists, then," he said dryly. "Perhaps I should have been more careful before firing you."

"I imagine you're always careful before you do anything."

"Sometimes my temper gets the better of my judgment." He glanced at her. "You must think we're a most belligerent family."

"Let's say I don't think I've seen the best side of any of you!"

His chuckle this time was louder and longer. "My life was extremely placid until Cathy and Celia came to live with me. Having a woman and child about the house made things much livelier."

"Did you find it disturbing?" she asked, curiosity overcoming the usual embarrassment she felt with him.

He nodded. "It was rewarding too. I enjoyed having a young mind to help formulate. Cathy was a bright child with an enormous capacity to learn."

"She's still bright, Mr. Lyon, though she's no longer a child."

His hands tightened on the wheel, and she was sorry she had introduced the present subject into their discussion. Had she not done so she might have learned more about his attitude and feelings.

"Let's not argue about my attitude to Cathy. Nothing you say will make me change my mind."

"You're so rigid!" she cried.

"So are you. And you're a romantic too. That makes it even more dangerous."

"What do you mean?"

"That you persist in seeing Alan through Cathy's rose-tinted glasses! She's spun you a yarn about his falling in love with her before he knew who she was, and you've swallowed it completely. If you could look at him objectively, you'd see him for what he was."

With an effort she kept a hold on her temper. "If you're still so much against him, why are you letting him see Cathy?"

"I've already told you. She mustn't have any stress. And if seeing him will help her to get better. . . . I'm also hoping that seeing him will bring her to her senses."

"You led me to believe there was a chance *you* might change your mind about Alan. But the way you're talking about him – "

"If I'd been completely truthful, you wouldn't have agreed to act as chaperone."

"I certainly wouldn't," she said hotly. "You deliberately led me to believe you had an open mind about Alan."

"I said I was willing to see whose opinion was right,' he corrected. "And I know *I'm* right!"

"You're the most pig-headed man I've ever met," she burst out.

"And you're the most pig-headed woman!"

With an angry stab on the brake he stopped the car, and Philippa shot forward, her head coming in sharp contact with the windscreen.

"Do you have to hurt everybody who comes in contact with

you?" she stormed. "Can't you be more careful what you're doing?"

"I'm sorry, I thought you were wearing your seat belt. Please forgive me. I never meant to hurt you."

His voice was strained, the words jerky, and her temper died as suddenly as it had sprung up. She rubbed the front of her forehead and felt a swelling beneath her fingers.

"You *will* be glad to see the back of the Lyon family, won't you?" he said in the same tender voice he had used to Celia, and then with a gesture that took her by surprise, he caught her shoulders and pulled her against his chest.

Despite the cold evening he was not wearing a coat, and through the fine material of his dinner jacket she felt the hammering of his heart and the warmth and strength that emanated from him. His arms around her were surprisingly weightless, and though his bulk made her feel she was in the clasp of a bear, it was an unusually gentle one. For such a big man he was amazingly light of touch. His chin rested on the top of her head and one hand came up to lift the fall of hair from her forehead and touch the bruised skin.

"You could claim compensation," he said whimsically.

"I'll suffer in silence."

"I doubt if silence is one of your virtues!" He held her slightly away from him, though she was still so close she could see the pupils of his eyes and the pale grey irises around them. It was like watching him on a television screen, with the camera lens trying to enter the heart of the man through his features. Yet his face gave nothing away, and remained as implacable and hard as she believed him to be. Yet not quite, for there was an unexpectedly warm look in his eyes and an unexpected tenderness in the way his fingers moved across her shoulders, gently kneading the flesh and reminding her of the gesture of a contented tiger.

Tigers and lions, she thought whimsically. How appropriate for this overwhelmingly masculine man.

"Feeling better?" he asked quietly.

"Yes, thank you. I'm sorry I lost my temper." She moved

away, oddly disappointed that he made no effort to stop her. "I never told Cathy that my trip to Thailand was cancelled." She said the first words that came into her mind, unwilling to talk any more about Alan. "She must have found out from someone else. I don't want you to think I bear you any grudge because of it."

"I'd never think that. You're not the type to bear a grudge."

It was the first nice thing he had said to her, and she felt as though the temperature had risen by several degrees; there was no other way to account for the warmth that enveloped her.

"Anyway, my firing you did cost you the trip," he went on, "and when Cathy suggested the Thai dinner, it seemed an excellent idea."

"You went to a lot of trouble and expense."

"It was only getting those damned lobsters. Everything else was prepared here."

"It was still nice of you to do it."

"Aren't you used to men doing nice things for you?"

She did not answer and his head tilted forward, the hair glinting silver in the light from the dashboard. "Don't tell me a hardboiled journalist can be embarrassed by a compliment?"

"So you *were* listening to the conversation at the table," she said involuntarily. "I thought you'd blanked out."

"I do when I'm bored or busy with problems."

"I had the impression you were bored at dinner tonight."

"Why should I have been?"

"Woman-talk," she said vaguely.

"With a few claws extended." Seeing her eyes widen, he smiled. "Celia's very protective towards Cathy and me."

Philippa was dumb-struck that he could be so blind. Did he really see his sister-in-law as protective of him? Protective of her own claim on him was nearer the truth.

"I can see disagreement flashing behind those golden orbs of yours," his voice was an amused growl in the back of his throat.

"We all see each other with different eyes," she said hastily.

"Meaning that you don't see my sister-in-law the way I do?"

His quickness discomfited her. "You know her better than I do," she hedged. "You're bound to see her differently."

"Celia doesn't appeal to other women," he conceded, "but she's done an excellent job with Cathy."

"I think *you* did it."

He slewed round completely and stared at her, then as though realising she had not been sarcastic, he rubbed the side of his face in perplexity. "I never thought I'd hear you say that to me."

"I know more about you now." She looked at her hands, wondering why they should have twisted themselves together. "Cathy talked quite a lot about herself this evening, and naturally you came into it . . . the way you encouraged her to think for herself – to use her mind . . . to make her aware of what's going on in the world."

"She has a good brain," he said. "That's why I want her to extend it. She's a fool if she rushes into marriage."

"Not if she's genuinely in love. Marriage needn't stop her from developing."

"How many married women do you know who still go on with their careers?"

"Plenty. Particularly if they can afford to have domestic help."

"No matter what help they have, they're still torn between two worlds. Between wanting to take care of their children and husband, and wanting to succeed in their career."

"Men have a home and family as well as a job."

"They're different from women," he asserted. "They don't feel guilty when they leave the baby and go to the office, but I've yet to meet a woman who doesn't want to rush home the minute her child starts crying for her. And don't say it's because she can't get help!"

"I wasn't going to. I agree with what you've said."

"That's a turn-up for the book! It's the first time you've agreed with me about *anything*!"

"It's the first time you've said anything valid."

He threw back his head and laughed, a loud sound that

echoed around her. "You don't go in for flattery, do you, Philippa?"

He had never called her by her name, and she wondered if he was aware of it.

"Philippa," he said again, answering her unspoken question. "The name suits you. It's sweet and sharp."

"I'm mostly sharp."

"But the sweetness is there, waiting to be tapped."

"You make me sound like a maple tree!"

"Your hair's the colour of maple syrup."

"Let's hope I don't come to a sticky end!" She tried to inject humour into a situation that was threatening to overwhelm her.

"Your end will be a house in the country, with dogs on the lawn and babies on the carpet!" He put a hand on the wheel and tapped it thoughtfully. "My niece and I seem to have invaded your life in the last few weeks. I hope we haven't caused too much disruption."

"I haven't a boy-friend to object, if that's what you wish to know," she said crisply.

"You don't believe in pretending, do you?" he said with a slight smile.

"Why should I?"

"Most women think it increases their desirability if a man believes other men are there ahead of him."

"I see no point in increasing my desirability with you." She stopped, realising too late where her words had taken her.

"You're right, Philippa," Marius Lyon said slowly. "You don't need to increase your desirability for me." He paused. "I already find you far too desirable as it is."

"Don't," she cried. "Don't *you* pretend!"

"Who's pretending?" As he asked the question he pulled her into his arms, and not expecting it, she had no defence ready. Not that any defence could have resisted the demanding passion of his kiss. There was no gradual build-up of emotion in it, only a white-hot intensity that enveloped and seared her. It was too sudden for her to respond to it, and she remained quiescent in his arms: a zombie into whom he was trying to breathe life.

His mouth lifted away from hers and he moved back slightly to look into her eyes. What he saw there seemed to satisfy him, for he drew her close and kissed her again. This time he did it with slow deliberation, kindling her emotions like the devil kindling his fires. His lips, his hands played their separate theme upon her until, senses aflame, she gave a convulsive shudder and put her arms around his neck, signalling her submission with parted mouth.

He did not take advantage of it, but continued to caress her with gentleness, encouraging her by his very control to lose her last remaining fear of him. She made no move to stop him when his fingers undid the buttons of her blouse, and as his hands cupped her breasts they swelled to his touch, making every part of her body ache with the need for him.

She had been kissed many times before with passion and urgency, but never had she responded with such abandon, nor had to fight so hard not to surrender completely. What was it about him that made her ache to respond to him, that filled her with an urgent need to caress his hair, to touch the thick column of his neck that rose from the burly shoulders? Perhaps the very strength and size of him made his trembling need for her all the more persuasive.

Again and again they kissed, his thighs pressing hard on hers, his hands warm on her body, moving across her back and down her spine, caressing her shoulders and spanning her waist: and all the while she felt his heart thudding against his ribs like a caged bird trying to escape its confining bars. She felt the dampness of his skin beneath her fingers, and only then did she discover that his shirt was undone and she was lying upon his bare chest, a strong chest with thick hair as soft as down.

"I hadn't anticipated this when I offered to drive you home." His voice was husky and almost inaudible.

"I'm glad it wasn't premeditated," she whispered back.

"I didn't think it would happen tonight," he admitted, rubbing the tip of his tongue along her ear. "But I wanted you the moment I saw you, I still do."

"You have a meeting to go to, remember?"

"I can cut it short," he said softly. "If I come back to you soon, will you let me stay?"

"Stay?" she asked, trembling.

"With you . . . tonight."

"No!" It was a sharp sound, louder than she had intended. "No," she repeated, more softly. "I've never . . . I couldn't!"

"Don't you believe in love?"

"Oh yes. That's why I . . . I mean it's because I do that I wouldn't want to anticipate it. I suppose you think that's stupid of me?"

"Extremely stupid in this day and age. But it's a stupidity I'm glad about." His arms came round her again, cradling her as though she were a child. "Darling," he said huskily, and then again, more urgently: "Darling!"

Once more his lips were on hers and Philippa gave him back kiss for kiss until the "No" which she had said so firmly a few moments earlier faded into insignificance, and every throbbing nerve of her body begged to be mastered. But the man seemed to remember her earlier assertion, and shakily he withdrew her hands from his neck and slid away from her.

"I've never seduced a woman in a car yet," he said jerkily, "but there's always a first time, and as you've made it clear that you won't. . . ."

With trembling hands she buttoned her blouse and smoothed her hair. "I think you should take me home, Mr. Lyon."

"So do I, Miss Rogers." The humour in his voice was pronounced. "After the last half-hour, don't you think you could call me Marius?"

Embarrassment washed over her. "It would seem strange. I've never thought of you like that."

"At least you *have* thought of me."

"Certainly," she replied. "And with quite a lot of dislike!"

A laugh rumbled in his throat. "You're not frightened of me, Philippa, that's one of the things I like about you." His hand came out and rested on her lap, warm and heavy, intimate in its pressure. "One of the many things I like about you."

He set the car in motion, and within a few moments they reached her block of flats.

"Don't bother getting out," she said quickly, "you must already be late for your appointment."

She jumped out of the car, but as she reached the entrance she found him beside her, towering above her in the darkness.

"Don't I get a goodnight kiss?"

"You've already had it." She tried to keep her tone light, but she was shaking so much that it was difficult.

"Do you ration your kisses?" he asked.

"Of course not."

"Then I'll take another." He bent his head to hers – it had to come a long way down – and softly kissed her brow. "Goodnight, my dear, sleep well."

She was standing by the lift when she heard his car drive away, and even when she could no longer hear the sound of it, it remained in her imagination as she pictured him driving through the darkness, steering fifteen thousand pounds' worth of luxury yet still managing to keep his pulse on everyday life. Therein lay the strength of his publishing empire: his ability to know what the public wanted and to cater for it, and his perspicacity in frequently being ahead of that public.

Undressing for bed, she paused to look at herself in the bathroom mirror. Tall and slender in a pale pink slip, with her hair falling to her shoulders and her face devoid of make-up, she looked like a schoolgirl. Yet there was nothing childlike about the languorous curve of her mouth, which still glowed red from the pressure of Marius's. What had happened to her tonight? A devil must have taken hold of her senses, otherwise she would never have responded to him with such abandon. One day – so she had thought – she would meet a man who would awaken her, who would make her fully aware of the pleasure of being a woman. But she had never believed it would be someone like Marius.

"No!" she cried aloud. "I'm mad. It isn't possible."

But it was more than possible; it was a fact. Hurriedly she

put on her nightgown and climbed into bed. She hardly knew the man. Nearly all their conversations had ended either in outright disagreement or barely concealed hostility. Even to-night, when he had discovered she had left Alan alone with Cathy, he had looked angry enough to hit her, yet only a little while later he had cradled her in his arms as if she were the only woman he wanted to hold, and she had lain against his chest as if that were the only place she wanted to be. As indeed it was.

In the darkness of her room she faced the incredible thought. She was in love with Marius Lyon.

"No!" she cried again, and sitting up in bed, switched on the light. But its radiance did nothing to dispel her wild imaginings, and one crazy idea after another kept crowding in on her.

Unable to remain in bed, she went into the kitchen to make herself a hot drink. She was a fool to have given her heart to a man who would never want to marry her. It was stupid to think he would. He was an important tycoon who wielded enormous power, while she had been an unimportant cog in his empire. What would a man like that have in common with her? He wanted to make love to her, but that didn't mean he was *in* love with her. It was a bitter thing to accept, especially when she herself wanted the depth of a real relationship, but not to admit the truth would be to live in a world of make-believe. They were a man and a woman with many years' difference of age between them and a vast abyss of experience separating them, who were nevertheless drawn together by the intangible yet steel bands of mutual attraction. It was nothing more than that, as far as Marius was concerned.

Thank heavens she was no longer working for him. Not that she needed to be in the same building in order to feel his presence. No matter where she was she was swamped by him: it was as if he could mentally reach out and draw her to him like a pin to a magnet.

Holding a cup of hot milk, she returned to the living room and switched on the electric fire; despite the central heating which gave uniform warmth to the atmosphere, she was shivering. What did she knew of Marius other than what she had learned from Cathy, who could never – under any circumstances – be described as impartial? Even so, her criticism of her uncle had been interspersed with eulogies: his benevolent despotism to his friends and family; his generosity to his brother – with whom he had nothing in common – and his prompt offer of a home to the widow and his niece when his brother had died. None of this suggested a man who was lacking in generosity, and it was not just generosity of money, but of time and thought. It would have been easy for Marius to have put Celia and Cathy in a house of their own, where he would not have been bothered with them except when it suited him. But aware that a fourteen-year-old girl still needed a father-figure to whom she could turn for advice and affection, he had opened his own home to her.

Philippa sighed. Marius's kindness had reaped him no rewards for now, four years later, he was regarded as a dictator by the one person whose love he had striven to obtain.

The warmth from the fire permeated her silk gown, and she relaxed in the chair, her legs beneath her, her arms folded across her breasts. How excited Marius had been by her nearness. It had been strange to know she could so easily arouse him, for she had assumed him to be a man of iron control: but even iron had a breaking point, and it was incredible to think this breaking point was her. But she mustn't go on thinking about him. To do so would lead to heartache, and to read too much into a few unexpected kisses was childish. How Celia Lyon would laugh if she could see her now, the so-called hardboiled journalist full of unrequited love, mooning about like a dying swan.

But how could she forget Marius if she went on seeing him? The guilt which he had aroused in her over Cathy was too strong to let her forget the girl's problems, and as long as Cathy was an invalid and needed her, she was obligated to make herself available.

A picture of him came vividly to mind, and he diminished the little room with his height and breadth. He was a man to inspire love and hate. Indeed he had done exactly that with her, inspiring first the hatred which had quickly died, and then arousing an unwilling admiration which had inexplicably turned to love. A love which, she knew with despair, would remain with her for ever.

CHAPTER TEN

Because she desperately longed to see Marius, Philippa used all her will-power to resist Cathy's pleading telephone calls and to come and visit her.

Her hope that she might hear from Marius died when the days passed without a word from him, though she could not stop herself from trembling every time the telephone rang on her desk. She had been a fool to think he would want to further their relationship. He was obviously not even sufficiently interested in her to try and have an affair with her! How bluntly he had asked if he could stay the night with her. Her body shook with mortification as she remembered it, and she was fiercely glad she had refused. How terrible she would feel now if she had not done so.

Unbidden, an errant thought came into her mind: what would have happened if she had said yes? Would she have had one night with him and then faced days of silence – as she was doing now – or would her surrender have awakened deeper interest that might have led to something more than one night of love?

Bitterly she acknowledged that the word love was wrong. A night of passion was a better way of putting it. If she had felt that love had prompted his desire to remain with her, she might not have found it easy to have turned him down.

On Friday she decided to go to Wiltshire to see her parents. She could not face the prospect of staying in London and going out with one of the young men who had asked her, nor did she look forward to her own company, and a return to her home seemed the natural solution.

As always, the grey stone manor gave her a sense of perspective and made the bustle of London seem light-years away. But if the well-loved pieces of furniture and the family portraits on the wall gave her contentment, they also made her realise she could not live her entire life alone, and she thought of all the men she knew and dismissed them one by one. How weak they were compared with Marius; weak not only in looks and physique, but in personality and achievement. Curiosity stirred in her about his background, and she wished she had taken more heed when Cathy had spoken of it. Firmly she pushed him from her mind and forced herself to listen to her father, who was regaling her with details of his long-standing row with a local farmer over a public right-of-way.

On Monday morning she returned to the office and learned that Cathy had called her three times. Knowing she would have to speak to the girl sooner or later, she decided to do it at once.

"A fine friend you are," Cathy said as she came on the line. "You go off with my uncle and I never hear from you again!"

"I've been busy," Philippa hedged.

"You were never too busy to come and see me when I was in hospital. You're not angry about anything, are you? Marius hasn't upset you, has he?"

"Of course not. What makes you say that?" Philippa did not realise how sharp her voice was until Cathy replied.

"Then he has upset you! Is that why you haven't been to the house?"

"Your uncle has nothing to do with it," Philippa lied. "I've already told you I've been busy."

"I wish I could say the same about myself. It's been like a morgue here, what with Marius in Australia and Celia mooning around like a ghost without a house to haunt!"

"I didn't know your uncle was away." Philippa's voice was studiously casual.

"He went the day after you were here. It was unexpected, I think. But don't let's talk about him. I rang up about Alan."

Philippa forced herself to concentrate on what Cathy was saying, but it was difficult, for all her thoughts were with Marius. So he had flown to Australia the day after he had taken her home! No wonder he had not called her this past week. And she had believed it was because he did not want to see her again. Of course there was no guarantee he would contact her when he returned home. He might well decide he did not want to see her again. She must be careful not to read what she wanted into his silence. Only time – and Marius's actions when he came back – would show her if she was hoping in vain.

"Are you still there?" Cathy asked.

"Of course I am. You were talking about your uncle."

"I was talking about *Alan*."

"What's wrong with Alan?"

"Nothing! But he's coming to see me today and you're supposed to be here. If you aren't, Marius will be furious."

"I never thought I'd hear you admit you didn't want to disobey your uncle!" Philippa said lightheartedly. Indeed it was amazing quite how lighthearted she felt.

"It isn't that I *want* to obey him," Cathy replied, "but if I don't, Celia will tell him. And if I don't see Alan on Marius's terms, I won't be able to see him at all."

"Stop worrying about nothing," Philippa replied. "I'll be over at six o'clock. Earlier if I can get away."

Her hopes of leaving the office ahead of time were doomed to disappointment. The unexpected arrival in London of a Hollywood film star with her seventh husband sent her to the Savoy to interview them, and the article she wrote so delighted Jack Lane that he decided to use it for the morning edition.

"Re-write the first page and let me have it," he ordered. "I'll take out the cookery column and put yours in."

"That *will* make me popular with the cookery consultant!"

Nonetheless she was delighted to know she would be getting her first by-line in the paper, and she spent such a long time polishing her opening paragraphs that it was well after seven before she had finished. Annoyed with herself for having been so slow, she telephoned Cathy to explain she would be late.

"I don't mind how late you are," Cathy giggled. "At least I've kept my word to Marius and asked you to come here."

"Has Alan arrived yet?"

"Five minutes ago. But don't worry, I'll be very good. You can be as late as you like."

Partly relieved and partly annoyed, Philippa put down the receiver. Much as she disliked acting as chaperone, she had given her promise to do so, and she felt guilty at not being able to carry it out. Undoubtedly Alan and Cathy were happier without her, but at the moment she was more concerned with her own peace of mind. Yet it was ridiculous for her to feel this sense of guilt. Was it because she loved Marius that she wanted to obey him, or was it because some part of her mind told her he might be right about Alan?

Hurriedly gathering together the typewritten pages of her article, she took it in to Jack Lane, waited for and received his approval, and then raced out of the building and flagged down a taxi. Alan might well have gone by the time she reached Belgravia, but at least she would be able to say she had put in an appearance.

It was half past eight when she entered the elegant hall of Marius's house, and not even pausing to give her coat to the butler, she sped across to the drawing room.

It was empty, and she stood uncertainly on the threshold. "I thought Miss Lyon and Mr. Bedford would be here," she murmured to the butler.

"Mr. Bedford has left and Miss Cathy has retired to her room." There was no expression in the discreet voice.

"Miss Lyon isn't ill, is she?" she asked quickly.

"I believe she was upset and went to bed."

"Do you think I might see her?"

The man glanced towards a closed door on the other side of the hall. "Please wait here a moment, miss. I believe Mr. Lyon wishes to see you first."

Philippa's heart gave a loud thump. Cathy had said Marius was in Australia.

"The master returned this evening," the butler explained, as though divining her thoughts, and then glided across the marble floor to the room opposite. He re-emerged almost immediately and inclined his head in her direction.

Nervous as a schoolgirl stepping into her headmaster's study, Philippa went in to see Marius. He stood up at her entrance but made no move towards her. His ruddy complexion was paler than she had seen it, with a grey tinge of tiredness emphasised by the darkness on his lids and the shadows under his eyes.

"I thought we decided not to let Cathy and Alan meet alone."

His voice was so harsh that it rubbed away her good intentions, and instead of agreeing with him, which she would otherwise have done, she tilted her head defiantly. "*You* decided, not me."

"Is that why you didn't obey me? You know damn well I won't have the two of them alone together!"

"Nothing will happen if they are!"

"How can you be sure?" He flung out his hand and she stepped back, afraid he was going to hit her, but it was just a gesture of fury. "He took Cathy out of the wheelchair and put her on his lap," he thundered. "If you think that's funny –"

"I think it's natural," she interrupted. "They love each other."

"He loves her money."

"You can't prove that."

"You can take my word for it. If Cathy had been an ordinary girl, he'd never have looked at her."

"Then disinherit her," Philippa burst out, and regretted the words the moment she saw the odd look on his face. "I didn't mean it," she said quickly. "I spoke without thinking."

"It's a good point nonetheless. I had already thought of it myself."

"You *couldn't* do it. It would be monstrous."

He sat down in a small armchair, completely filling it with his bulk. "What do you think Cathy's position would have been if her father hadn't died?" he asked coolly.

The question took Philippa by surprise. "I don't know. I suppose you'd have just been the rich uncle who sent her a magnificent wedding present."

"A little more than that, perhaps," he conceded, "but she

certainly wouldn't have been an heiress. It's only since she started living with me that I began to regard her more as a sister than a niece. It seems to me that if Arthur was alive today, she wouldn't have had to worry whether or not her suitors wanted her or her money."

"*Must* you put it like that?"

"Are you squeamish about talking of money?" he asked sarcastically. "The middle classes often are."

"I just don't like the way *you* talk about it." She turned away from him, fighting back the longing to burst into tears. So many times since their last meeting she had told herself not to cherish foolish hopes about him, but never had she envisaged that when next they met they would be quarrelling as though they had never been in each other's arms. Certainly he did not seem to remember it. She forced herself to look at him again. "If you've finished chastising me I'll go."

Her words had an electrifying effect on him, for the colour rushed into his face, making his complexion ruddy again, and he jumped out of the chair and came over to her in one long stride. "My bloody temper!" he exclaimed. "It's the first time I've seen you since – and I spoil it by shouting at you." His hands came on to her shoulders and gave her a little shake. "But it's your own fault. You've a nasty habit of pulling the lion's tail!"

"That's not true," she retorted, too afraid to show him how happy she was. "You were furious with me before I even came into the room, and even more furious once you saw me," she said, puzzled.

"Because it made me realise how much I've missed you. You've been too much in my thoughts, Philippa, and I don't like it."

"Then put me out of them."

"Were you able to forget *me*?" He saw her answer in the colour that rushed into her face, and gave a triumphant laugh. "It looks as if we're both caught, doesn't it?"

She nodded, her eyes starry. "The only difference is that I don't mind, and you do." She waited, hoping he would deny it, but instead his hands dropped to his sides and he moved away from her. "You look tired," she said.

"I feel it. Tired and old." He flexed his arms as though he found his clothes restricting. "Tired and old," he repeated.

"You should have a hot bath and go to bed," she said, before she could stop herself.

"Alone, or with you?"

"You'd be very surprised if I said with me."

"I'd just think you were using a woman's privilege and changing your mind." As always he was getting the last word and it made her faintly mutinous.

"Why do you want me, Marius? You can have so many women without having to ask twice."

"Perhaps I find it a change, having to ask twice. Man is a hunter, don't forget. He likes the thrill of the chase."

"You're talking in clichés."

"Because your question was trite! You don't need me to tell you why I want you." Again he was close beside her, his warmth almost tangible. "You have a beautiful body – the little I've seen of it – and a lovely face."

"Is that all you want of a woman – a body and a face?"

"Until now it has been enough." He paused, frowned and then went to stand by a tray that stood on a satinwood secretaire next to the window. "What will you have?" he asked.

"Nothing, thank you." She tried to keep the disappointment from her voice. "I haven't eaten, and if I drink on an empty stomach I'll – "

"Cathy didn't say you were coming to dinner," he interrupted.

"I had expected to be here at six o'clock, but I had to finish an article." She looked him squarely in the face. "I did intend to be here with Alan. It was just unfortunate that I wasn't able to manage it."

"It seems I owe you an apology."

"I don't expect you to apologise."

"Why not?"

"Have you ever done so?"

"Not since I was a child," he admitted. "But I've no objection to apologising if I am in the wrong." One large hand came out and touched her cheek. "I'm sorry, Philippa; sorry I lost my temper and sorry I misjudged you."

She forced a smile to her lips, and aware that she could not control their trembling, moved away.

He looked at her in silence, then returned to the table and poured himself a whisky. "I'm nearly forty," he said suddenly. "Don't I seem old to you?"

"Only when you ask a question like that!"

He did not show any amusement, and leaned against the mantelpiece, surveying her seriously.

"Please sit down," she begged. "I can't bear you towering over me."

"Do you want me to lose all my advantages? I'm doing my best to keep you in your place."

"What is my place?" she demanded.

"The cradle, as far as I'm concerned. You're a child, Philippa, like Cathy."

"I'm four years older than your niece, and light-years older when it comes to experience."

"So?"

"So *you're* being childish when you talk to me like this." She lowered her eyes to the carpet and debated whether to continue, deciding that if she did not do so, she would regret it when she was alone. "When you took me home the other night – when you kissed me and I. . . ." She focused on the carpet more intently. "Did you think I kissed you back as if you were my father?"

"For heaven's sake!" he burst out. "What are you trying to prove?"

She willed herself to raise her head and look at him. "That I – that I think you're the most attractive man I've ever met."

He set his glass on the mantelpiece and with slow deliberation came to stand close to her. One hand cupped her face while the other pushed the hair back from her forehead. "The face of a child," he murmured. "That full mouth, the little nose, even the way your forehead curves: a baby face."

"I didn't kiss you like one," she whispered, and before she could stop herself, put her arms around his neck.

Her touch was his undoing, and he gathered her close, lifting her completely from the ground. It was her first experience of his strength and she revelled in it, arching her body against his and twining herself close against him.

"Philippa, no," he said huskily.

"I should be the one to say that," she teased, and had no opportunity to say more, for his mouth covered hers and made words impossible.

She was not conscious of time; all she knew was that she was swept along on a wave of feeling that made coherent thought impossible. It might have been seconds or moments later when he gently disengaged her arms and held her away from him.

"We'd better have something to eat," he said huskily. "I'm sure it's hunger that's making me shake."

"It's *me*!" she retorted.

His large head tilted, and the look he gave her was quizzical. "You're very daring all of a sudden. Aren't you scared of me any more?"

"Not when we're here. If we were outside my flat it would be another story!"

He chuckled, and going to a telephone picked it up, pressed a button and ordered supper for two. Then he came back to sit in the armchair opposite her. "I understand you haven't been here since I last saw you."

"I've been busy."

"You've generally found time to see Cathy."

She bit her lip and then decided to be partially truthful. "I felt I was becoming too involved in your affairs. I know I promised to be here whenever Alan and Cathy met, but I – I hope you'll release me from my promise."

"I won't." It was a flat statement.

"But I'm a stranger and I feel in the way. Why can't Mrs. Lyon be there instead of me?"

"Because Cathy regards *you* as her friend."

"A young 'Aunt Jessie'," she said crossly.

"It *was* your advice that helped to precipitate the whole thing."

"That's the only reason I agreed to be here," she flared.

"Is it? Is it *only* guilt that binds you to the Lyon family?"

She was glad that the arrival of the butler with a trolley prevented her from having to answer. The cold supper provided was resplendent enough to suit the most demanding palate; a mound of caviar with small, hot buckwheat pancakes on which it could be piled; a tureen of creamy soup with button mushrooms floating on its surface and a crystal bowl of strawberries, frosted with sugar. Hunger at the sight of such food overcame her embarrassment at eating alone with him for the first time, and she piled her plate high.

"I'm glad you don't peck at your food," he said, filling his own plate.

"I probably would if I had to worry about my figure."

"Don't you?"

"I never think of it."

"I wish I could say the same. I've thought of nothing else since I first saw you!"

She went scarlet and concentrated on a pancake.

"You're a strange mixture of innocence and sophistication," he said quietly. "You flame up like a peony when I least expect it, and you're all over the top of me when I anticipate you hiding yourself behind the settee!"

"What a thing to say!" she exploded, and seeing his broad smile, began to giggle.

He joined in slowly, as though he was not used to laughing with anyone, and she was suddenly struck by the feeling that he must have led a lonely life until Cathy and Celia had come to live with him. A life full of business friends and love affairs, but with no one person with whom he could totally be himself. Still, she was sure it was not because he had been unable to find the right person, but because he had not wanted to do so. Marius was a loner, ploughing his own field with single-minded purposefulness.

The meal seemed to relax him and some of the fatigue left his

126

face. But that he was still tired she could tell, for he was content to sit quietly without making conversation, his lids occasionally closing. Philippa could have sat opposite him for ever, savouring the sight of him and the pleasure she felt in being close to him, but she was conscious of the exhausting journey he had just completed and at ten o'clock she stood up.

"You're tired, Marius. I'll go and see Cathy for a few minutes, and then go home."

"Cathy was given a sedative before you came."

"Was she ill?"

"She was hysterical. When I arrived home and found you weren't here, I sent Alan away. Cathy got excited about it and – " He shrugged and did not finish the sentence.

"I wish you hadn't made a scene," Philippa sighed. "For someone so clever, you've no idea how to get your own way peacefully."

"Do you think I enjoy fighting with Cathy?"

"Then you should try and be more diplomatic."

"The last time I was diplomatic she ended up by eloping. She's wilful and headstrong, and if I let her get the bit between her teeth she'll gallop away."

"You can't keep her tied up for ever."

"Only until she's learned enough to know I'm right." He stifled a yawn. "Don't quarrel with me, Philippa, I'm too tired."

Instantly she was contrite. "You should be in bed."

"I'll go as soon as I've taken you home."

"I wouldn't dream of letting you drive me home. It's just as easy for me to take a taxi."

"No," he said decisively, and went with her to the door. As he opened it, the front door opened too and Celia came in, elegant in a black velvet dress and coat that heightened her silvery fairness.

"Marius!" she cried, and running forward, raised her lips for his kiss. "We weren't expecting you until tomorrow. Why didn't you let me know? I'd have come to the airport."

"I didn't know myself." His kiss was affectionate and he kept his arm over her shoulder. "You look very well, Celia."

She gave him a gentle smile and moved slightly closer, turning to look at Philippa as she did so. "Have you been with Cathy?"

Philippa shook her head. "I was delayed at the office and got here late. Cathy was already in bed."

Sensing a deeper implication behind the words, Celia looked at Marius.

"Cathy and Alan were alone together when I got back," he said quietly. "Philippa hadn't arrived yet and you were out."

"Lady Baxter asked me to have dinner with her. I wouldn't have gone if I'd known Miss Rogers wasn't going to get here in time." The grey eyes rested balefully on Philippa. "You should have telephoned to let me know."

"I didn't realise it would cause such a disaster." Philippa was unsuccessful in hiding her irritation. Both Celia and Marius were making a mountain out of a molehill, and her sympathy for Cathy grew even stronger.

"You don't know my stepdaughter as well as I do, Miss Rogers."

"Philippa and I have already talked about it," Marius came into the conversation as though he sensed Philippa's temper. "I'll get my coat," he said to her, "and take you home."

"I wish you wouldn't," she said again. "I'd much rather get a taxi."

"Where's Thomas?" Celia asked.

"I sent him home."

"Then I'll take Miss Rogers."

Marius stifled another yawn. "Would you?" he asked gratefully.

"Darling, of course." Celia's hand came up and touched his cheek. "Miss Rogers is quite right, you do look exhausted."

"It's the change in temperature, as well as time." He turned and looked at Philippa. "We'll meet again."

It was not the most satisfactory goodnight she could imagine, but she kept a smile fixed to her lips as he got into the lift and closed the door behind him. It glided away and Celia crossed to the front door.

"There's no need for you to drive me home either," Philippa said quickly. "I'll get a taxi."

"Marius wouldn't like it."

They went down the front steps and Celia unlocked the door of a silver-grey Mercedes coupé. "He doesn't like women going out at night unescorted. When you consider some of the magazines he publishes," she added, switching on the engine, "he's rather surprisingly old-fashioned."

"You mean he preaches one thing and practises another."

Celia nodded and concentrated on driving, which she did very well. "I know you think Marius and I are wrong in our attitude to Cathy, but you really shouldn't judge us without knowing the whole situation."

"I just think she isn't a child and shouldn't be treated like one."

"But she *is* a child. That's what you don't seem to understand. She has led an extremely sheltered life. She was fourteen when her father died, but if you had seen her, you would have thought she was ten."

"She's grown up quickly in the intervening years," Philippa's voice was dry.

"Outwardly only. Inside she's still an infant."

Philippa glanced at Celia, wondering how much she meant of what she said, and how much she said because it suited her. But the sharply-cut profile gave nothing away.

"My only regret," the woman went on, "is that Cathy's such a burden to Marius. He's been so wonderful to her, and to me, too."

"Do you like living in England?" Philippa asked, feeling she was expected to say something.

"It's my home now. I couldn't imagine living anywhere else, especially as Marius and I – " She stopped speaking and the car purred on in the silence. "He's a wonderful person, you know, Miss Rogers. I realise you've had arguments with him, but to those he loves – "

"He has a strong sense of family," Philippa concluded in her most detached voice.

"Exactly! That's one of the things I meant when I said he was old-fashioned. He thinks the family unit has the greatest social importance. I suppose it's because he comes from a broken home."

"I didn't know that."

"His father disappeared when he was two and Arthur was ten. Their mother earned a living by cleaning offices. It's the sort of story you read about and never believe could actually happen. It makes his success that much more wonderful, of course. Arthur won a scholarship to a private school and was then semi-adopted by a clergyman and his wife, but Marius remained with his mother and left school when he was fourteen. All his education came from night school when he was in his twenties."

"I've read about that part of his life," Philippa said involuntarily, "but I didn't know about the early part. It explains why he's so ambitious. There's no motivation stronger than a man's desire to give his mother all the comfort she never had when he was a child."

"He was devoted to her," Celia agreed. "I always think that's why he never married."

"Mr. Lyon doesn't strike me as being mother-fixated," Philippa said dryly.

"I didn't mean any complex reason like that." The reply was swift and positive. "I meant it's made him look for a wife with much the same qualities she had; and because he couldn't find them he wouldn't take second best."

Remembering many of the society beauties and film stars whose names had been linked with his, she could appreciate why he had found it difficult to find someone with his mother's qualities. Nor was he likely to find them among the bevy of names with whom he was currently linked.

"That's why Marius was pleased when Cathy and I came to live with him," Celia went on. "It gave him a family again."

"He should marry and have a proper one," Philippa said before she could stop herself.

"He's going to – very soon." The pale blonde head turned

130

sharply. "Please forget I said that, Miss Rogers. Talking with you like this I – I forgot you're a journalist."

"I'm here as Cathy's friend," Philippa said coldly.

There was a deep sigh. "Please don't be annoyed with me, but I've been rather indiscreet talking about Marius and myself, and. . . ." Again there was a hesitation, and when Celia spoke again it was to change the subject entirely and to ask which turning they should take as they drove into St. John's Wood.

Philippa must have given the correct answer, though she was not aware of having spoken, so shattered was she by the quietly devastating words Celia had spoken. Was Marius really going to marry this self-satisfied woman who, according to Cathy, had married her father as a means of putting herself into Marius's life? The thought of such premeditated action was horrifying, indicating as it did an almost manic determination that would brook no interference. She glanced at Celia surreptitiously. Could she have been lying? Was she deliberately insinuating that she was going to marry Marius in order to establish her claim on him?

Philippa sighed. The only way she could disprove what Celia had said was to ask Marius directly. But she would never do that. He was not the sort of man who allowed his motives to be questioned. Besides, she had no right to question him. A few kisses – no matter how passionate – were not the open sesame to his heart.

Yet later, as she lay in bed, she wondered exactly how Marius felt towards her. He certainly desired her, but did it go beyond that? Remembering the companionable ease with which they had sat together tonight she longed to believe there was something deeper between them, but her intelligence would not allow her to do so. Marius was a man of the world, used to women's attentions, and it would not require any effort on his part to be completely relaxed with a young girl like herself, and all the more so if he knew she loved him.

Mortification washed away her confidence, and she floundered on a sea of bitter memories, all Celia's words coming back to haunt her. "Marius was pleased when Cathy and I came to live with him . . . he was part of a family at last. . . . Marius and I. . . ."

"No," Philippa cried aloud, and buried her head in the pillow. "It should be Marius and me — Marius and *me!*"

CHAPTER ELEVEN

Morning sunshine brought a resurgence of Philippa's confidence. Celia's remarks to her in the car were not as important as the ones Marius had made when they had been alone together having supper, and it was these words which remained with her as she went to the office.

"Pleased with your article?" Sandra Sinclair – one of the other Feature writers – asked her as she came in.

"I haven't seen it yet." Philippa dived for *The Monitor* and turned to the Features section, where her interview with the middle-aged star had been given pride of place. Hastily she scanned it, delighted that very little had been subbed.

"And your name in inch-high type too," Sandra added. "If it had been me I'd have waited up all night for the first edition."

"I forgot all about it."

"You must be in love!"

"I am."

"Really?" Sandra's pert face was eager with curiosity. "Is he a journalist or does he work for a living!"

"He's in Fleet Street," Philippa grinned, "but you don't know him, and I'm not going to tell you his name either, so get back to your desk and direct your big eyes at your typewriter!"

Good-naturedly Sandra did as she was told and Philippa looked at the telephone, wondering if Marius would ring her or whether – if he didn't – she would dare to call *him*. But what would she say to him if she did? She couldn't tell him she loved him. She frowned, trying to envisage his reactions if she did exactly that.

"When's the happy day?" Sandra asked from the other side of the room. "Or is it the sort of love that won't lead to marriage?"

"I don't know if *he* loves me," Philippa muttered.

"Like that, eh? Lots of touch and tenderness, but nothing put into words!"

"Plenty of words," Philippa corrected, "but open to all kinds of interpretation."

"He sounds a clever one."

"He is. Clever and experienced."

"Then watch out. He isn't married already, is he?"

Philippa shook her head. "Lots of affairs, but nothing permanent."

"What makes you think *you're* likely to be?"

"I don't think it," Philippa said desperately. "I'm just hoping and keeping my fingers crossed."

"Keep your other boy-friends as well. That way you won't cry your heart out if it comes to nothing."

Like most good advice this was difficult to follow, though Philippa kept repeating it to herself as the day passed without a word from Marius. She had lunched with a young crime reporter who had been one of her most persistent admirers since meeting her three months ago, and though she tried to pretend an interest in him, she had stared into his face and only seen Marius, so that the effort to concentrate on what he was saying had finally given her a headache and she had been thankful to return to the office. Some girls might be able to love a man and yet play the field, but she was not one of them. It was a sobering thought, but it made her realise there could be many months of misery – if not years – ahead of her. Yet she must not let herself think like this. She hardly knew Marius. If she did not see him again she would forget him in a few days. After all, there was nothing unusual or wonderful about him. He was intelligent and handsome, but so were many other men. He was rich, of course, and could give a woman everything her heart desired; yet she would love him if he were poor and could not give her anything. "I do love you," she cried silently. "Marius, Marius. . . ."

The telephone rang and she snatched it up, expectation dying as she heard Cathy's voice insisting she come over at once.

"I can't, I'm busy." Not for anything was Philippa going to present herself at Marius's house tonight.

"You've got to come," Cathy cried. "Alan's going away and it's all because of you. My uncle was furious because you weren't here and he – "

"I've already spoken to him and told him why."

"Did he tell you what he was going to do?"

"About what?"

"About Alan." Cathy was shouting, her voice thick with tears. "He's making him go to Australia!"

"Don't be silly. Your uncle can't make him do that."

"You don't know Marius," Cathy said bitterly. "He can make anyone do anything. Anything! He's got power and he doesn't care how he uses it as long as he gets his own way." She began to cry. "If Alan goes, my whole life's a waste!"

Sobs made the rest of her words indecipherable, and full of fear, Philippa promised to come and see her at once.

Speeding across London in a taxi, she found it difficult to think clearly; she refused to think clearly, in fact, determined not to judge Marius without hearing his side of the story.

Hardly had she entered the black and white marble hall when a wheelchair came hurtling towards her, its occupant tense and white-faced. "I'll never let them part me from Alan," Cathy shouted. "I'll follow him if I have to do it on my hands and knees!" She burst into noisy sobs and Philippa hurriedly propelled the chair into the drawing room and closed the door.

"For heaven's sake, stop being hysterical," she said in her most cutting tones. "Tell me what happened."

The sharpness did the trick, for Cathy hiccoughed, stopped crying, and blew her nose. In jerky but intelligible sentences, she explained what had happened, part of which Philippa already knew. Marius had returned from Australia unexpectedly last night and had found Alan and Cathy alone in her bedroom. He had almost thrown Alan out of the house and had then gone down to wait for Philippa's arrival.

"It was stupid of you to have taken him to your room," Philippa said.

"We only went in case Celia came home," Cathy explained, "but Marius was furious about it. He was mad with you too, but

135

you know that, if you saw him last night."

"He cooled down pretty quickly," Philippa retorted, "and he never said a word about Alan going to Australia. I'm sure it isn't *his* doing. He can't force Alan to go. The days of the press-gang are over!"

"Whose side are you on?" Cathy wailed.

"Yours, of course, but I still can't believe what you've told me." She came closer to the girl. "Are you sure your uncle's sending Alan away? I mean, why should Alan go, if he doesn't want to?"

"Because Marius has made him believe he'll be doing it for *my* good. He's told him I might not be able to walk for years and that I'll need expensive treatment and looking after. He says if Alan doesn't stop seeing me, he'll throw me out!"

"He'd never do that."

"He's made Alan believe he will." Tears started to fall again, "That's why he's going to Australia. He won't even come and see me before he leaves."

The tears turned into a flood and Philippa, impotent to do anything to stop them, felt her anger against Marius rise. But she had to control it. She had to know all the facts before she could judge him

"Perhaps *you* can make Alan change his mind." Cathy was speaking again, her voice rough from crying. "I *will* walk again! I know it. The physiotherapist was here this morning and she agreed with me." Cathy threw the blankets off her legs and pointed. "Look, I can move them!"

Philippa stared at the thin feet, already beginning to waste after two months' inactivity, but though she looked hard she could see no sign of movement

"I can flex the calves," Cathy said fiercely. "Put your hands on the back of my legs and feel."

Philippa did so and felt the sudden bunching of muscles beneath her fingers. "That's wonderful," she murmured, "but you mustn't get excited. "It's only a beginning."

"But it *is* a beginning. That's what I'm trying to tell you. I'm

136

going to be Alan's wife no matter what Marius says. He's the only boy I've ever loved."

"You're not nineteen yet," Philippa reminded her. "You've got your whole life ahead of you."

"I won't fall for anyone else – if that's what you're hinting," Cathy retorted. "You've got to make him change his mind. He *can't* go to Australia."

"Why should he listen to me?"

"Because if you tell him I'll walk again, he'll believe you. Please see him for me," Cathy begged. "I'd go myself if I could walk."

Still Philippa hesitated, and seeing her reluctance Cathy's anger returned. "Are you frightened of what Marius will say? Do you have to obey him as if you haven't got a mind of your own?"

"Of course I don't."

"Of course you *do*," Cathy taunted. "You're as bad as Celia. She fawns all over him too. You're both cut from the same mould."

This fighting speech was enough to rouse Philippa's wrath, and though she knew she was reacting to Celia's name like a bull to a red rag, she could not prevent herself. "Very well, I'll see Alan for you, but afterwards I'll talk to Marius." She glanced at her watch. "Where will Alan be now?"

"At the garage, I think."

An hour later Philippa arrived at the address which Cathy had given her. It was more of a repair depot for racing cars than a regular garage, and several men in oil-stained dungarees were either lying under engines or bent over them. But there was no sign of Alan and when she asked where he was, the foreman told her he had already left.

"Not just for the night," he added. "He's gone for good. Said he was off to Australia in a few days."

The neutrality which Philippa had been trying to maintain lost some of its strength. If Marius had been able to arrange for Alan to leave so quickly, he must have been planning this for a long time. That meant it had been in his mind even while he had agreed to let him and Cathy meet.

"Did Alan say why he was going?" she asked casually.

"Said he had the chance of a job that would lead to racing. He's dead keen on racing, you know. It's his life." The foreman's eyes narrowed. "You a friend of his?"

"I'm a friend of the girl he was engaged to."

"Never knew he was."

Philippa hesitated. "Could you let me have his address? I can't contact his fiancée – she's out of town – and I have to see him urgently."

The man rummaged through some papers on his desk, then jotted down an address. "Here you are, miss. Catch a bus outside; it'll drop you almost at his door."

Following the instructions, she was soon presenting herself to a prim-faced landlady who ushered her into an overcrowded front parlour before going in search of Alan.

After a moment he sauntered in, flushing slightly as he saw who his visitor was.

"If you've come to make me change my mind about Australia," he said at once, "forget it. I'm going."

"But why? If you love Cathy – "

"That's why! What life can I give her? At least if she's with her uncle he can give her what she needs."

"She needs you!"

"She has to have proper care." he said fiercely. "All the things I can never give her in a month of Sundays."

"She won't always be an invalid," Philippa insisted. "She'll walk again."

"She won't! She's kidding herself."

"She can move the muscles in her legs."

"That means nothing. She'll be in a wheelchair for years." He sighed. "Tell her to forget me. We were crazy to think we could ever get married."

"You eloped with her once."

"Look what happened to her," he said roughly.

"Is that why you're running away? Because you blame yourself for the accident?" He nodded and her sympathy for him grew. "I feel guilty too," she went on, "but *I'm* not leaving her in the lurch."

"Stop it!" He sat down and buried his head in his hands. His slight shoulders were moving, but for a long while he did not speak. "It's no good," he said at last. "My mind's made up. I'm going."

"Won't you at least see Cathy to say goodbye?"

"It will make it worse. Tell her I love her but she must forget me."

Philippa went to the door and with her hand on the knob, turned to look at him. "Was it Mr. Lyon who found you the job in Australia?"

"Yes."

"Is sunshine more important to you than Cathy?"

He did not answer and she walked out.

In the street she stood uncertainly. A meeting with Marius was indicated, though the thought of it was abhorrent. But it was impossible to return to her flat; there were many things that needed clarifying and until they were, she would have no peace of mind.

Once more she returned to Belgravia, and walking past the elegant houses, thought bitterly of the different ways in which power could be used: to build or to destroy, as Marius was now destroying.

With his usual impassivity the butler ushered her into the hall, and at her request to see his employer, led her to the drawing-room.

Marius was pacing the floor, the look on his face indicating that he had been doing so for a long time.

"I had a feeling you would be back," he said.

"You know where I've been?"

"Cathy told me."

"Why didn't you tell me about Alan last night?"

"I only spoke to him today. Until I did, I wasn't sure what I was going to do."

"That's a lie!" she burst out. "You knew exactly what was

139

going to happen. You have always wanted to part him from Cathy. You may pretend you didn't in order to gain time."

"Don't make judgments before you know the whole story."

"I know as much as I need to! Cathy and Alan love each other and – "

"Not that again," he interrupted.

"Why not? It's the truth."

"It isn't." He shook his head. "Alan's going to Australia and Cathy will get over him."

"What if she doesn't?"

"She will."

"Just because *you* aren't capable of loving," Philippa flared, "it doesn't mean other people aren't!"

"I haven't forced Alan to go," Marius stormed.

"Of course you have." Philippa was furious and made no attempt to hide it. "You said you wouldn't take care of Cathy unless he did. If that isn't force, I don't know what is."

"You're very quick to believe the worst of me."

"I believe what's true. You *would* stop looking after Cathy if she went off with Alan. You'd let her remain an invalid for life if she wanted to marry someone of whom you didn't approve!"

Marius took a step towards her. His colour was ruddier than usual and his eyes glinted like silver-grey daggers. "You enjoy believing the worst of me, don't you?"

"I believe what my heart tells me."

"What your heart . . ." His hand moved in an odd gesture. "It tells you I would do all the things you've just accused me of?"

"Yes."

He turned his back on her and remained like that for several moments. She stared at his impeccably cut jacket – which in no way diminished the massive shoulders – and the thick grey hair that lay close against his neck. She longed to run over and tell him she did not mean what she had said, but to deny the truth now would not prevent it from returning to haunt her later, and she clenched her hands and forced herself to remain where she was.

At last, when she was debating whether to leave, he turned and looked at her. He was calmer than she had ever seen him, his face devoid of expression.

"Since my niece is no longer seeing Alan, there'll be no need for you to act as her chaperone." Even his voice was expressionless. "So if you don't wish to see her again. . . ."

"Are you telling me I mustn't?"

His thick grey brows almost met in a frown. "No," he said slowly. "She may well need you in the next few months, and if you could see your way clear to remaining her friend . . . as long as you keep out of my way."

"You needn't worry about that," Philippa said icily. "I'm as loath to see you again as you are to see me."

"In that case – " he turned and sat in a chair. "Cathy's in her room," he said without looking at her. "I assume you'd like to see her now you're here?"

"Yes, please."

"I'm sure you'll both have a wonderful time discussing my shortcomings."

"There's no point in discussing someone who doesn't exist," she retorted. "You're not a person to me, Marius, you're a newspaper tycoon with a printing press where your heart should be!"

"You're still fond of clichés, Philippa."

Angrily she went out and banged the door behind her.

CHAPTER TWELVE

For the next two months Philippa's nerves were strung to breaking point. Her desire to make a new life for herself was thwarted by the knowledge that she could not desert Cathy, and though her meetings with the girl brought Marius constantly to mind, she saw no way of avoiding them.

She had not seen him since their quarrel, if such a one-sided row could be designated as such, and reliving the scene she knew he had neither defended nor explained his actions. He had merely acted as if he believed in the divine right of kings; because he wished it, then so it must be. She had only to think of this again to tremble with rage. But unfortunately rage could not eradicate love, and though she hated him, she still ached for him; though she despised the very thought of him, she was still sick with the longing to feel his touch.

She grew thinner and paler, but it suited her, making her look like a model, so Sandra Sinclair said. She decided to take advantage of the fact and spent the increase in salary which Jack Lane had given her, by buying a mass of new clothes, all more sophisticated than those she generally wore. She had her hair re-styled too, cutting it to ear-length so that it swung provocatively against her cheeks and lifted like a cloud when it was touched by the slightest breeze or movement of her head.

Only her parents remained unfooled by her changed appearance, and though they did not question her, their awareness of her unhappiness kept her away from them, forcing her to fill the lonely weekends in other ways. Because of this she started to go out with the men she met, but none of them helped her to forget Marius, and coming home to her flat after an evening of dining or dancing, she would fling herself on her bed in a passion of tears and wonder how long her need of him would continue.

It was crazy to go on wanting a man who did not exist. Her imagination had given him a character that was alien to him, turning a shadow into a substance, and it was the substance for which she was aching.

In an effort to see him as she now knew him to be, she spent hours reading through all his press cuttings in *The Monitor* library. Many different women had been linked with him, sometimes for months, sometimes only for weeks, then were replaced by another famous name or glamorous face. It said much for his canniness that there was never a whisper of an engagement or impending marriage to be read in any of the hundreds of inches of type written about him. Side by side with his amorous affairs she read of his business ones, one successful *coup* following upon another as he turned from provincial newspaper tycoon into national one, and through it all he remained smiling enigmatically, his hair as thick at forty as it had been at thirty.

The sight of him, even in a picture, was always her undoing, and she would fold the cuttings away and return them to their file, vowing never to look at them again, but inevitably returning to read more of his exploits and to bring herself up to date with what he was doing.

Deliberately she refused to let Cathy talk about him, and sensing that if she did, it could terminate their friendship, the girl rarely spoke of him, though there were many occasions when Philippa came to the house and found her in a mutinous rage – due either to something he had said or to arrangements he had made for her welfare.

Because of the embargo she had placed on speaking about him, it was only through the Fleet Street grapevine that she learned *The Monitor* was being bought by Lyon Publications, and on Monday morning she went to the office to discover she was once again Marius's employee.

"All our jobs are secured," Jack Lane told her, calling her into his office. "He's bound to make changes, of course, but it's up to us to make sure they don't occur in the Features section."

He hesitated and Philippa's mouth went dry. Why had Jack called her in to see him? Had Marius ordered him to fire her? Knowing she detested him, she would not be surprised if he had.

"How would you feel about taking over the 'Dear Jessie' page?" Jack enquired, and seeing her astonishment, added: "Kennedy Jones just rang and asked me. Mrs. Hibberd's definitely going and the big white chief himself suggested you."

Philippa could not believe it. That Marius himself should put forward her name was so incredible she knew there must be a logical reason for it. Could it be guilt over his earlier dismissal of her, or was it merely his way of showing her how little she meant to him? Certainly it indicated that he no longer had any objection to having her work within the precincts of his own building.

"Don't turn it down," Jack advised. "I know you want to do general features, but if Lyon himself suggested you...."

"I'll talk to Kennedy before I decide," she murmured.

"Go and get it settled now. And if you decide not to take it, think up a good excuse!"

Half an hour later she was in Kennedy's office, being greeted like a long-lost friend and handed an official contract showing her what her new salary would be.

"Why such a substantial rise?" she asked, looking at it.

"Orders from the top." There was a speculative gleam in Kennedy Jones' eyes. "I hear you're a friend of his niece?"

"You know how that came about," she said stiffly.

"Jessie told me. What's Lyon like on his own ground?"

She shrugged. "I haven't seen him for months."

"I heard you were very friendly with him. Thought you'd be his next 'good friend', as a matter of fact."

She forced a grin to her lips and nonchalantly sauntered to the door, murmuring that there were several things she wanted to talk over with Jessie. "I'm still not sure about doing the column," she warned, "so don't count on it."

"You'll be daft if you don't. It's a chance of a lifetime."

It was a sentiment which Jessie Hibberd echoed, though she did not belabour the point, and instead commented on Philippa's appearance. "You'd do well as a cover girl for *Vogue*, my dear, but if you get any thinner they'll be using you on the front page of *Spirit World*!"

Philippa laughed and hugged the woman, wondering fleetingly

144

where she would be now if Jessica Hibberd had been in the office that night when Cathy had come calling. Quickly she pushed the thought away.

"So you're finally going to retire?"

"I'd have done it months ago if you hadn't left."

"I was fired," Philippa said. "Don't pretend you've forgotten."

"I doubt if I'll forget. But at least Mr. Lyon's making amends for it. Don't let pride stop you accepting the offer."

"It's not pride," Philippa was reluctant to say more, but knew she had to say something. "I see quite a bit of Cathy still, but I – I don't see Mr. Lyon. We had a quarrel and. . . ."

"Then let's not talk about him." Mrs. Hibberd opened a drawer in her desk and took out an enormous bundle of letters. "There are some interesting problems among these that I think you should write about once you take over the page."

"Oh, Jessie," Philippa choked, "if only everyone was as understanding as you!"

That night Philippa decided to write Marius a thank-you note. He had offered her the position because she was a good journalist, and she should acknowledge his action. It was foolish to see any personal motive in what he had done. Indeed, the fact that he wished her to work on his own paper again was a clear indication that he no longer saw her in any personal way. Yet even if she remained on *The Monitor* she would still be working for him, though she had to admit that coming back to *Today's News* seemed to bring him closer. She smiled wryly. Considering that she saw Cathy at his house each week yet never so much as glimpsed a sight of him, she was hardly likely to do so in an office block the size of Buckingham Palace! Pushing personal thoughts of him aside, she penned him a brief note and posted it. He had shown her that he could put business first, and she intended to show him she could do the same.

Carrying the step to its logical conclusion, she coolly told Cathy of her new position, and was surprised to find that the girl already knew of it.

"Marius said he was going to offer you the job."

"I didn't know you were on speaking terms with him!"

"I heard him tell Celia. I was eavesdropping," she said brazenly.

Philippa bit back the impulse to know if Marius had said anything else about her. Cathy might be egocentric, but she was suspicious of anything concerning her uncle, and might well read a great deal in even the most casually framed question. Regretfully she decided to change the subject, but before she could do so Cathy spoke again.

"Celia was talking to him about you. That's why I listened. She doesn't like us being friends, you know." The dark eyes were speculative. "Perhaps it isn't your friendship with *me* that's worrying her. It could be Marius she's – "

"Your uncle and I aren't friends," Philippa interrupted.

"You interested him. I could tell from the way he watched you."

"You're as imaginative as your stepmother. I haven't seen him for months."

"Since Alan went to Australia," Cathy muttered, and her pale face, which had grown more peaky of late, looked older than its eighteen years. "I still love him, Philippa. Not seeing him hasn't made me forget him."

"You must try. After all, he went away because he believed he was doing what was best for you."

"He went because Marius forced him."

"There's no point discussing it. You can't change the situation, so you should learn to live with it."

"Who says I can't change it?" Cathy threw aside the blanket covering her legs and lifted first one and then the other. "Who says I can't change the position?" she repeated triumphantly. "I've not told anyone yet, but I'm starting to walk."

"Since when?" Philippa gasped.

"More than a week. Miss Evans wanted to tell Marius, but I've sworn her to secrecy. She thinks I want to wait until I can surprise him by running downstairs to greet him."

"Don't you?" Philippa asked, knowing the answer she would get.

"You can bet your life I don't!" Cathy retorted. "The minute

I can stand on my own feet I'm going to Alan. A month from now – two months at the most – and we'll be together."

"Have you written and told him?"

"No. If he knew I had his address he might leave Sydney. I'm going to wait until he can see me for himself, till his own eyes show him I'm not an invalid and that we won't need Marius's money to make me well again."

Philippa wondered if she should try to dissuade Cathy from her plans. Not that the girl would listen in her present mood. She watched as Cathy re-covered her legs with the blanket. There was no doubt that her desire to be with Alan had spurred her on towards greater effort in following all the physiotherapist's instructions. Whatever Marius said about Alan, he would not be able to deny this.

"You won't tell Marius about my being able to walk?" Cathy asked anxiously.

"You know I won't. I think you should tell him yourself."

"No! Never."

"What are you being so adamant about?"

A husky voice made them both turn to see Celia coming into the drawing room. As always she was elegantly and expensively dressed, her blonde mink coat echoing the colour of her hair.

"What are you being so adamant about, Cathy?" she repeated.

"It's none of your business."

Colour seeped into the matt skin. "Just when I begin to think you're becoming an adult you act like a child."

"Isn't that what you want? As long as I'm a baby you can force Marius into giving you a home. You should go out and get yourself a job," she said rudely. "Living a life of luxury's making you fat."

Celia ignored the comment and looked at Philippa with commiseration. "I don't know how you can bear to come here."

"You'd like her to stay away, wouldn't you?" Cathy said furiously. "But it won't help you to catch Marius any more quickly. He'll never marry you!"

"Don't be too sure."

There was a knock at the door and the butler came in to say

147

that the car was ready.

"Thank you," said Celia, as gracious as a queen. "I'll be out in a moment."

"Where are you going?" Cathy asked.

"Marius is giving a dinner for the directors of *The Monitor* and I'm acting as hostess. You see what I mean about not being so positive? Because you don't want something to happen, it doesn't mean you have the power to prevent it." She went to the door and paused to look back at Philippa. "At one time I had hoped you would help my stepdaughter to become a more mature personality, but I'm afraid it's a lost cause!" She closed the door behind her, leaving a silence that was tangible.

"Bitch!" Cathy muttered.

"So are you," Philippa said mildly.

"I thought you didn't like her?"

"I don't, but that doesn't mean I think you're right to be so gratuitously rude."

The wheelchair moved restlessly on the carpet. "Marius can't be stupid enough to fall in love with her."

"She's elegant and attractive," Philippa forced herself to say.

"She's ice-cold and hard."

"So are a lot of the other women he's known."

"Known, yes," Cathy retorted, "but never wanted to marry."

"How do you know?"

"He once told me. He said he's never asked anyone to marry him."

Philippa tried not to retain the words, for they brought him so vividly to mind that it became a physical pain.

"Why are you frowning like that?" Cathy demanded.

"I was trying to envisage your uncle being married," she said truthfully. "If you really don't like Celia, you should be pleased if she marries him."

"Why?"

"Because he'll give her a rotten life. He's autocratic and domineering and – "

"Don't be daft," said Cathy. "He'll make a wonderful husband."

"Providing his wife is willing to be a slave!"

"Don't you believe it! He may be tough on the surface, but he's a marshmallow inside."

"Are you sure we're talking about the same person?" Philippa queried, keeping her voice light in an effort to check her emotions. "I take it you *are* referring to the man you were ranting about a moment ago?"

"I only hate Marius when I think of Alan," Cathy confessed, and sent her chair gliding to the far side of the room. It came to rest beside a table and, gripping the edge of it, she began to ease herself up.

Heart pounding, Philippa watched as Cathy slowly got to her feet. One thin leg moved forward on the floor, followed after half a moment by the other; then both began to move forward in ungainly, shuffling steps.

"See," Cathy said triumphantly. "I can walk!"

Tears blinded Philippa's vision, and she ran forward and caught the younger girl close. "Be careful," she begged. "Don't do anything silly."

"I know exactly what I'm doing. All my plans are made."

Philippa drew back. "Would you like to tell me?" she asked carefully.

"Not yet. Wait until I can walk properly. Then you'll find out."

When Philippa next saw Cathy, no reference was made to her physical condition, and reluctant to start a conversation that would inevitably lead to Marius and Alan, Philippa kept all discussion centred on her own work. Luckily it gave her a great deal to talk over. The "Aunt Jessie" page was now called "Talk Over", and Philippa found herself being invited to speak at schools, Women's Institutes and on television chat shows. Several times she had known that her youthful and glamorous appearance had caused surprise, but once she began to talk – usually from well-prepared notes – she was able to command respect, and with a dozen successful lectures behind her, the confidence which she had at first assumed soon became real.

Her initial fear that she might accidentally meet Marius in the office had disappeared, and she no longer looked apprehensively around as she walked through the reception hall to the lift, or down the long corridors as she went from one office to another.

Only as Christmas approached did he again loom large in her thoughts, for he always gave a staff party for his leading writers and, as she had anticipated, she received an invitation too. Knowing it would cause comment if she didn't go, she debated whether to take a few days off before the party and pretend she had 'flu. It was an easy way out, but it smacked of cowardice, and determined to put herself to the test and prove she had got over him, she returned her invitation card marked in the affirmative.

"These shindigs usually finish at midnight," Robin Summers informed her over lunch a few days before the party. He was News Editor on the paper: the youngest man ever to have held the job. Philippa had met him on her return to *Today's News* and they had immediately formed an undemanding yet companionable relationship. Of late he had intimated his willingness to take this further, but when she had not responded to the suggestion he had not pressed it. There was one good thing about having a boy-friend who had a highly demanding job: it absorbed so much of his energies it gave him little strength or time left for the chase. The thought made her smile, though she was unaware of doing so until he remarked on it.

"Care to share the joke, Jessie?" It was his favourite name for her, and one he used when he wanted to tease.

"I was thinking how lucky I am to know you."

"I'd like to know *you* a bit more. Still set on being a single-minded career girl?"

"He travels fastest who travels alone."

"He could still join forces for an occasional weekend."

"Ask me again in six months – if you haven't found someone else by then."

"I won't find anyone else." He leaned across the table, his narrow face quizzical. "Don't forget you're coming to the party with me. What time shall I pick you up?"

"As late as possible."

If he was surprised by her remark, he did not show it, though she immediately regretted having spoken, for it was impossible to explain that she wanted to arrive when the party was in full swing because it lessened the risk of Marius talking to her on his way around the room.

But Robin did not forget her remark, and on the evening of the party he did not call for her until eight. The look on his face as she opened the door to him told her that the money she had spent on her dress had been worth every pound, and confidence surrounded her like a shield as she went down with him to his small red sports car.

"A News Editor should drive something more respectable," she teased.

"That remark, coming from a girl in a topless dress. . . ."

"It isn't topless!" she protested, and looked down at the neckline. "Is it?"

"I wouldn't let you hitch it up one single millimetre," he said cheerily. "You look stunning. I've never seen you in black before."

He drew her hand to his lips and a tremor went through her, though it was not for him that her body cried, but for the man she would soon be seeing, the man for whom she was wearing this drift of black chiffon.

Arriving at the Savoy and entering the private banquet hall, her heart hammered so loudly in her ribs that she did not hear what was being said to her and accepted a glass of champagne from Robin and made a pretence at gaiety. No one noticed anything odd about her behaviour as they moved from one group of people they knew to another. As always the talk was "shop", and rival papers and rival reputations were made and destroyed with equal rapidity.

"Let's see where we're sitting," Robin suggested, and drew her over to the table plan set up on an easel outside the main doors.

Too nervous to concentrate on searching for her name, she let Robin do so, and watched him as he looked down the list. He was handsome, she thought involuntarily, rather like an older edition of Alan, but stronger-looking. The hair was the same blond colour and he had the same ease of manner, but his chin was firmer and his grey eyes more intense.

"We're next to the top table," he said, "spitting-distance from the Lord High Chief himself."

The glass shook in her hand and champagne spilled.

"Watch out," said Robin, and took hold of it.

"My hand slipped," she apologised. "I'd better not drink any more on an empty stomach."

His look was searching but he made no comment, and she was grateful to him. He knew she was a friend of Cathy's and that she went each week to Marius's home, yet he had never questioned her about it, nor commented on the gossip that had surrounded her return to *The Monitor*.

"Don't turn now," Robin whispered, "or you'll tread on the lion's tail!"

Philippa stiffened like a corpse, but there was no change of expression on her face, though she could not have spoken had her life depended on it.

"Hello, Robin," a deep voice said. "That was an excellent piece you wrote in the paper yesterday. I meant to call and tell you, but I knew I'd be seeing you tonight."

"I'm glad you liked it, sir." Robin took the compliment in his stride and, still in command, attempted to take command of Philippa. His hand under her elbow was warm and firm as he turned her gently but forcefully round to face Marius.

Philippa's eyes focused on a broad expanse of shirt-front, then helplessly travelled up to rest on the wide, thin-cut mouth.

"Good evening, Philippa," said Marius. "How do you like being back on *Today's News*?"

"One paper is very much like another." Was this her voice speaking, she wondered desperately, this shaky thread of sound?

"Printer's ink can't run in your veins, then," he replied. "A true journalist will go to the gallows for the paper he works for!"

"Perhaps women take longer to build up a loyalty." She marvelled at her ability to reply intelligently, but breathed a sigh of relief when two men joined them; one spoke to Robin and the other to Marius, leaving her free to her thoughts. She held them at bay like an animal on the defensive, but was suddenly aware that Marius was no longer talking to anyone and had come to stand beside her.

"How are you?" he asked, so low that only she could hear.

"Working hard." She looked at the sharp white collar around his neck. It was slightly too loose for him and she knew it was deliberately so. Regardless of fashion, Marius was not a man to let himself be confined.

"You still come to the house." It was a statement, not a question.

"You haven't ordered me not to do so."

His jaw tightened, but when he spoke there was no anger in his voice. "Given enough time Cathy will forget Alan."

Philippa said nothing and Marius too remained quiet. She glanced at Robin and saw he was still immersed in conversation. Desperately she wondered if she could rush off to the cloakroom, but decided instead to stand her ground. She drew a deep breath, and was aware of Marius lowering his head. She felt rather than saw his eyes rest on the curve of her breasts and wished desperately for those extra few millimetres.

"You're looking particularly lovely tonight," he said quietly.

Only then did she raise her eyes to his. It was a shock to look into them and see herself reflected there, and she felt as though she were sinking into their depths. With an effort she pulled her eyes away from his.

"You're politer now than when we last met," she said coldly.

"I was angry with you."

"And now?"

"Time heals all wounds."

"Does that mean you've forgiven me?"

"It means I understand why you were angry. I was foolish to expect you to understand me; we're a generation apart."

Over his shoulder she saw Celia coming towards them. Fury swept over her and she lashed out at him, "I can see my mother approaching."

His eyes narrowed. "Your mother?"

"Well, she could be," Philippa said sweetly. "She's the same generation as you!" This time the hiss of his breath was audible and he swung round as Celia reached his side.

"Hello, Philippa," Celia trilled. "I wasn't sure if it was you. You look so sophisticated, doesn't she, darling?" This to Marius who again looked at Philippa.

"Don't be misled by appearances," he replied. "She's as much a child as Cathy."

Again Philippa glanced at Robin, and as if aware of her distress he moved over and put an arm around her waist, at the same time shaking hands with Celia, whom he was meeting for the first time.

"Marius has told me how clever you are," the woman said charmingly, "or isn't it diplomatic me to say so?"

"It's always diplomatic to say nice things to people," Robin smiled. "That's what these sort of get-togethers are for: mutual back-scratching with no claws showing!"

"It's time we did a bit of back-scratching with other people." Marius's voice was lazily amused as he put his hand on Celia's arm and moved across to another group.

"That leaves me free for the rest of the evening," Robin murmured. "Now we can enjoy ourselves."

Philippa wished she could endorse the remark, and knew she had made a mistake in hoping to brazen her way through this evening. What a fool she had been to hope that seeing Marius again would make her realise she did not love him. Her first sight of him had told her the stupidity of such a hope; whether she liked it or not, he would always be a part of her life, an unfulfilled part that would forever remain an oasis of desolation. Her eyes searched for him, not that they had to search hard, for he loomed head and shoulders above everybody else. Under the light of a glittering chandelier his hair looked more silver than she had remembered, and as he half-turned and glanced momentarily at her across the room, she knew her memory had not played her false. He was greyer, the hair at his temples almost white.

Deliberately she pulled her eyes away and gave Robin such a widely beaming smile that he responded to it by drawing her close.

"Let's go to our table," he suggested, "and avoid the crush."

She followed him to their places. Other people were already doing the same, and within a few moments Marius and the other directors seated themselves at the top table. By an unfortunate mischance he was seated almost opposite her, and she had only to raise her eyes from her plate to stare directly into his face. The first time she did so their glances met, and from then on she was careful not to look in his direction, focusing her attention instead on Robin.

Eventually the meal was over, the speeches were made and dancing began. Marius and Celia took the floor first, followed almost at once by the other directors and their wives.

"I assume that's the sister-in-law," Robin murmured in Philippa's ear, as they too began to dance.

"Yes. She's Cathy's stepmother."

"And future step-aunt, would you say?"

"Could well be." Philippa nestled closer against Robin, willing herself to think only of him.

He responded by resting his cheek on hers, and she closed her eyes and pretended they were other arms around her. The music stopped and there was a polite spattering of applause, then the tempo changed and became slower. Robin went to catch hold of her again, but a black-clad arm came between them, and with something like despair Philippa knew what was going to happen.

"Proprietor's prerogative," Marius said easily, and waltzed Philippa away.

"I don't want to dance with you," she said in a tight voice.

"I prefer unwilling women. Or don't you like being reminded of the last time I held you?"

Amazed at his cruelty, she refused to show how much he was hurting her. "It's a waste of time remembering things that are finished."

"I don't think we did finish. I've often regretted that." He twirled her round. "Haven't you?"

155

"It might have made a good story for my children," she retorted. "It's always nice to boast that you've had an affair with your boss."

"It's not too late."

She pulled back in his arms and tilted her head to look at him. His mouth was set in a tight line and there was something vicious in his eyes. "Why are you trying to hurt me, Marius?"

His eyes moved over her as though removing the chiffon, and she felt herself grow warm beneath the intensity of his gaze. In this crowded room, with its bright lights and loud music, they still seemed to be in a world of their own.

"Beautiful young women always provoke me," he said thickly. "Particularly if they still remain a challenge."

"Would it have helped if you had possessed me?" she asked bitterly.

"Is that an offer?"

She drew a shuddering breath, and at that moment Robin danced past with Celia. "Certainly not," she said brightly. "I'm engaged to Robin."

There was no change on Marius's face, yet she felt the tremor in his hands and knew she had taken him by surprise. "He's a lucky man."

"I'm lucky too. He's just the person I've been looking for." She was chattering aimlessly, saying anything that came into her head. "He'll probably want me to stop work, so you'll have to find someone else to run 'Talk Over'."

"I can't see you as a *hausfrau*."

"I want babies," she said clearly. "Lots of babies. You should get married too, Marius, or you'll be too old."

Steel glinted in his eyes. "It's the age of the mother that matters – and Celia's only thirty-three."

Philippa stumbled. "When's the date?"

"That's what I wanted to talk to you about."

This time she stopped dancing, only starting again as he pulled her close. "What has it got to do with me?" she whispered.

"I want to send Cathy on a cruise. She's constantly at loggerheads with Celia and the quicker they're apart the better."

"I assume you intend to get married while Cathy's away?"

"Yes," he said quietly, "but I'd appreciate your not mentioning it to anyone."

"Not even to Cathy?"

"To no one." He drew her to the side of the floor. Several people moved respectfully out of the way and they were left alone, half-hidden by a tall green plant. "Cathy needs a change of air," he continued. "I've booked a suite on the *Tanberg Castle* for a round trip to South Africa. It takes about six weeks. I was hoping you'd go with her."

"*Me?*"

"I hadn't realised you were engaged to Robin, but I'm sure he can manage without you for a short time."

"No," she said quickly. "He wouldn't like it at all."

"I'll talk to him."

"No," she said again. "It's more than that. I don't want to go."

He was silent for a moment. "Cathy needs you," he said finally. "She won't go unless you do."

"I can't live my life around Cathy. It isn't fair of you to expect me to."

Moisture glittered on her lashes and seeing it he lowered his head towards her. "Why are you upset? You like Cathy, don't you? Why should you object to going with her, so long as Robin doesn't mind?"

Philippa closed her eyes, wondering what he would say if she told him that all she objected to was the knowledge that while she was away with Cathy he would be marrying another woman. "I have my own life to live," she said huskily.

"Surely you can spare six weeks?"

"And what happens when Cathy comes back? Will I still have to dance attendance on her if she needs me?"

"She won't be needing you, except as a normal friend. She's getting the feeling back in her legs. In a matter of months she'll be walking." He saw Philippa's eyes widen and he smiled. "Cathy's not very good at keeping a secret. She thinks I don't know. . . ." He gave a heavy sigh. "Both of you treat me like a fool."

157

"I don't," she began, and then stopped, knowing he was partially right. "Cathy wants to surprise you," she said lamely, and felt terribly guilty as she saw the sudden relief in his face.

"Is that why she hasn't told me?"

"Yes. She – wants to wait till she can run down the stairs to greet you."

It was as if a weight were lifted from him and he threw back his head and laughed. "I should have guessed. A woman's mind works in such a strange way. . . ." He hesitated. "About the cruise. . . . I hope you'll think about it."

"I will; but I'm not making any promises." Behind them the music stopped, and with relief she saw Robin coming towards them. "Darling!" she cried, and stretched out her hands to him, aware of Marius watching her as she moved into the circle of Robin's arms.

"You looked as if you wanted to be rescued," he murmured.

"Were the distress signals so obvious?"

"No more than Celia Lyon's," he grinned. "She was as anxious to get to the big boss as you were to leave him."

Desolation swamped Philippa, and she was gripped by a momentary depression that was paralysing. "Let's leave. I've had enough of this party."

"Are you sure it's the party?"

She turned away. "I'll get my coat."

Not until she was sitting beside Robin in his car was she able to breathe more easily, and as they sped along the Embankment she lowered the window and savoured the cold night air.

"You're in love with Marius Lyon, aren't you?" Robin said, as prosaically as if he were discussing the weather. "I always suspected it, but tonight I was sure."

She glanced at his profile and, sickened by all her subterfuge, knew it was time to be truthful. "Yes, I am."

"Poor darling." His hand clasped hers. "If there's anything I can do to help?"

"No one can help me," she said fiercely. "I'll get over it in time." She gave a half sob. "Marius once said I use too many clichés. It's true. I suppose, but I can only think of a cliché at the moment."

"Like time healing all wounds?" Robin asked. "It does, dear Philippa, it does."

CHAPTER THIRTEEN

Seeing Marius again revived all Philippa's love for him, and one sleepless night succeeded another, causing her to grow visibly thinner and paler.

"If you lose any more weight you'll disappear," Robin said one evening as he came to her office to take her to dinner. "Perhaps you should go on that cruise, after all. Mr. Lyon's willing to let someone else write the column and – "

"If it were only the cruise!" she cried, and burst into tears.

"Hey there, what's all this about?" Robin drew her close and patted her head. "Tell me, Philippa, it'll do you good to get it out of your system."

She hesitated, reluctant to show Marius in a poor light and equally unwilling to disclose Cathy's plans.

"Tell me," Robin insisted. "News editors always get their story in the end!"

She gave him a watery smile and moved out of his hold. She was aware of him watching her as she wiped away her tears, but he made no attempt to encourage her to confide in him. His silence was somehow comforting, and glancing at his face, serious and full of concern for her, she decided to take his advice and confide in him. He would not be able to change the situation, but at least telling him would make her feel she had an ally.

Haltingly she began to speak, and once she started the words poured out. "Cathy has no intention of going to Africa. She's planned for us to leave the boat at Le Havre and fly to Australia. That's where Alan is – the boy she wants to marry." As concisely as she could, Philippa told Robin of Cathy's previous elopement, of her accident and of the threat Marius had used to make Alan leave England. "He said he'd stop paying for Cathy's treatment if Alan didn't go. That was why Marius and I quarrelled."

"It was a despicable threat to make," Robin agreed. "Are you sure he did so?"

"He never denied it. It was the only way he could force Alan's hand. But now Cathy is able to walk, she's going after him."

"Doesn't Marius guess?"

"He thinks she's just beginning to regain the use of her legs. He's got no idea that she's almost completely recovered."

Robin pulled at his lower lip. "And she's making you a party to the whole scheme?"

"What else can I do? Marius insists I go with her on the cruise, and if I tell him what she's planning, she'll never speak to me again."

"Would that worry you?"

"Not really," Philippa said with honesty, "but I can't give her away. It would be sneaking."

"Mr. Lyon might consider you were being disloyal to *him* by not doing so."

"He doesn't deserve any loyalty. I hate Marius for what he did."

"Hating him is one thing; conniving with Cathy is another."

"What else can I do?"

"I'm not sure. I'd like to meet Cathy, though. Why don't we go along there this evening?" Seeing Philippa's hesitation, he said: "Do you have set visiting hours with her?"

"Of course not. But I always go on a specific day and Marius knows it. That way we don't meet."

"Be a devil and take a chance on it," Robin urged. "After all, I'll be with you."

"Very well." Philippa smiled at him. "I feel much better now I've told you the whole story. I wish I'd had the sense to do so before"

"So do I. It might have stopped you looking like a skeleton."

"Am I as bad as that?"

"A sexy skeleton," he corrected. "It emphasises your breasts."

"Stop it!" she admonished, suddenly too happy to be embarrassed, and clung to his arm as they left the office.

It was not until they were driving to Belgravia after dinner that she asked him if he had any plan in mind regarding Cathy.

"I'm going to tell her I know what she's up to, and pretend

161

I'm on her side," he said.

"And then?"

"I don't know. One thing I *am* sure of, though, is that Mr. Lyon didn't behave the way you think he did. If he believed his niece was genuinely in love with this Alan, he'd never do anything to hurt her."

"He's a domineering man and he wants his own way," Philippa said tautly.

"He's an emotional man and he's obstinate," Robin corrected, "but he's also kind." He stopped the car outside the white, corner house and followed Philippa up the steps.

She had telephoned to say she was coming and Cathy, still in her wheelchair, was waiting in the sitting room to greet them. Watching her play the part of hostess, Philippa was surprised by the girl's charm; given a little longer to mature, her personality would be delightful.

Robin seemed to think so too, for within minutes he and Cathy were talking together as if they had known each other for years. He introduced the subject of Alan by saying he was a racing enthusiast too, and had seen Alan several times at Brand's Hatch. This made Cathy even more expansive towards him, and when he and Philippa stood up to leave, she begged him to come and see her again.

"She's a sweet girl," he commented as they left the house and drove away.

"Now perhaps you can understand why I can't tell Marius what she's planning to do. I'd feel a beast if I ratted on her."

He nodded. "It's a pity I can't see the boy-friend. Then I'd have some idea why Mr. Lyon doesn't like him."

"I've told you why. He thinks Alan's after her money."

"Do you?"

"I don't know. I'd probably give him the benefit of the doubt; which Marius won't, of course."

"Mr. Lyon's a canny business man." Robin changed gears. "That doesn't mean he's infallible, though. It might be an idea if I. . . ." He lapsed into silence and they drove for several miles without either of them talking.

Finally Philippa broke the silence. "Do you have any plan in mind, Robin? That *was* the whole point in your meeting Cathy."

"Something's beginning to gel," he muttered, "but I'd like to keep it to myself for a bit. Do you mind if I don't answer you for the moment?"

"Not at all. Providing you promise not to tell Marius what's going on."

"I'm no sneak either," he smiled.

During the next fortnight Robin came with her whenever she went to see Cathy, and on the fourth occasion Philippa definitely felt herself to be *de trop*, for the two of them made no attempt to draw her into their conversation and were soon deep in a discussion of poetry and literature.

Cathy was wearing her hair differently tonight, the long dark strands being pulled away from her face into a French pleat. It emphasised the pure line of her cheeks and made her look older, though at the same time more vulnerable. She was wearing a new dress too, and no longer had the blanket over her legs. Watching them, Philippa was struck by the quick affinity which had sprung up between them, and wished she had had the foresight to bring Robin here before. Perhaps if she had, Cathy wouldn't be making arrangements to go to Australia.

A sudden draught of air made her turn, her heart fluttering in her throat, but the beat subsided as she saw it was Celia. For an instant the woman looked at Robin blankly, then recognition dawned, and after greeting him with unexpected warmth, she settled herself next to Philippa.

"Is he your latest?" she asked lightly.

Philippa nodded. She was reluctant to lie, yet in view of what she had told Marius the night of the party, she could not say the truth.

"Wedding bells seem to be in the air," Celia remarked.

"I know. I'd like to – to congratulate you. Marius told me about your engagement. He asked me not to say anything to Cathy, of course."

"I see." Celia's heavy lids lowered, masking her eyes. "When did he tell you?"

"At the party."

"You must have been upset."

"Why should I have been?"

"Because I know how you feel about him." There was compassion on Celia's face. "You've made it very obvious."

Scarlet-cheeked, Philippa turned her head away. To have Celia's dislike was bearable; to have her pity was insupportable.

"Just because *you're* in love with Marius," she said coldly, "you shouldn't assume *every* woman wants him."

"But *you* do. There's no need to pretend with me."

Philippa fought for self-control, and pride helped her to win the battle. "Marius is an attractive man and well-known. It isn't surprising that I was flattered by his attention, but I never thought of him in terms of marriage." She forced herself to smile. "He's too old for me anyway."

"If you say so." The reply came in a disbelieving tone and Celia stood up and glided away.

Too restless to remain where she was, Philippa stood up too. "I'm going out for a breath of air," she explained, and aware that Robin and Cathy had not even heard her, almost ran from the room.

Wrenching open the front door, she stood on the steps enjoying the cold air on her skin. From the road came the flash of headlamps and the purring of cars, while in the distance she heard the chime of a clock. A few more cars flashed by and then one came to a stop, by the kerb.

Trembling, she recognised Marius's Rolls, and watched as he stepped out of it. There was a weariness about him she had not seen since the night he had come back from Australia. He did not look happy either; no one would think he was planning his marriage. Perhaps his tiredness came from overwork and his efforts to clear things up in order to take a long honeymoon. Angry at her thoughts, for she did not care what he did with his life, she went to step back into the house, but he had seen her and strode up the steps.

"You don't usually come to see Cathy on Friday. Is anything wrong?"

"No. But Robin wanted to see her and this was his only free night."

"You mean he's here with you?"

"Of course." She was fiercely glad she could give him this answer. "Where else would he be?"

"Have you reconciled him to your cruise?"

She nodded and stepped into the hall. Marius took off his coat and dropped it on a chair. "Which room are you in?"

She pointed to the small sitting room, and with a curt nod he walked past her and entered the drawing room.

Blinking back her tears, she rejoined Cathy and Robin, wishing she had had the sense never to leave them.

"It's a pity you can't come to Australia with us," Cathy was saying as Philippa came in. "We'd make a marvellous foursome."

"I don't think Philippa would fancy being squired by Alan," said Robin.

Cathy stared at him and went scarlet. "You know I didn't mean *that*. Honestly, Robin, I – "

"You haven't been honest for years," he teased. "You're a born liar, even to yourself."

"That's a horrid thing to say." Cathy's temper, always at trigger point, rose.

"I'll amend the word 'liar' to 'actress'," Robin said easily. "You love dramatising yourself and people take you seriously."

"How much do you charge for your analysis?" Cathy asked with asperity.

"A kiss," he replied, and bending down, took one. When he straightened, Cathy flung Philippa a questioning look.

"Don't mind me," Philippa grinned. "Robin and I are just good friends, and I do mean *friends*! You're more than welcome to him."

"I'm in love with Alan," Cathy said furiously, glaring at them both. "If you think it's fun to flirt with me – "

"It's more than fun," Robin intervened, "it's exhilarating!

165

Let's see if a second kiss is as good."

"If you touch me again I'll scream!"

"If you do, and your uncle comes in, I'll tell him of your nasty little plan."

"You wouldn't dare!"

"Try me." Deliberately he bent and kissed her again, but on the forehead this time, with his hands on her head. "You're a darling girl, and when you grow out of your puppy love for Alan, I'll be waiting for you." He sauntered over to Philippa and winked. "Let's go."

"Don't come back!" Cathy called.

"If *I* don't, Philippa won't, and you can't manage without her if you're going to go on your supposed cruise."

"You're a beast!" Cathy stormed.

"That's why women love me," he agreed, and hastily pulled Philippa from the room as Cathy wheeled round in search of something to throw.

"I suppose there's method in your madness," Philippa remarked when she and Robin were alone.

"I was testing Cathy's reactions to a kiss."

"And?"

"And it was surprisingly responsive for a girl who's supposed to be in love with someone else."

"She needs affection," Philippa said seriously. "Don't misjudge her response."

"I'm not." He was equally serious. "If Mr. Lyon hadn't been so pig-headed, Cathy would have got over Alan long ago. It's only because she's as obstinate as her uncle that she won't even admit to herself that she might have changed her mind."

"But she does love Alan," Philippa persisted. "I've seen them together – you haven't."

"You've seen *us* together, too."

Philippa was at a loss. There was truth in what Robin said. She had noticed Cathy's response to him and her changing attitude in the last couple of weeks. Yet the girl still insisted upon going to Australia. The tickets were bought and the plans were made.

166

"It's ten days before you leave," Robin said, when she reminded him of this. "A lot can happen in that time. *I've* made some plans too."

"I wish you'd tell me what they are."

"I will when I come back."

"Where are you going?"

"On an assignment. I'll be away several days. I'm leaving tomorrow, actually."

"I'll miss you."

As Philippa kissed Robin goodnight and entered her flat, she realised how much she had meant her last remark. She could never love Robin, but at least when she was with him her loss of Marius was more bearable. A picture of Marius came into her mind; his thick grey hair and broad shoulders; his hard mouth which could become so soft and tender. Soon that tenderness would be Celia's and those broad shoulders would pillow her silver-blonde head. The knowledge was so devastating that she sank down in a chair and buried her head in her hands, praying for strength to live through the next few weeks before she and Cathy left London.

The thought of all the subterfuge that lay ahead filled her with dread: the pretence that they were going to remain on the boat, the mad dash to the airport once they reached Le Havre, and then the long flight to Australia with heaven knew what at the end of it. Yet Cathy seemed confident that everything would work out well, and Philippa prayed that it would, pushing away her disappointment that Robin had been unable to offer her any advice or help.

His absence left a blank in her life, but she resolutely refused to go out with anyone else, finding it less wearing to be on her own and wallow in self-pity than to pretend to a gaiety she did not feel.

On the third evening Cathy called unexpectedly to see her, brought by the chauffeur and deposited in an armchair. Not until the door closed behind the man did Cathy stand up. She was still slow in her movements, but she was walking better every day.

"What a fraud you are," Philippa expostulated. "Letting the poor man carry you in when you can walk as well as he can!"

"Marius has made me a fraud," Cathy retorted. "Where's Robin?"

"Away on a job."

"He's not a reporter."

"He still goes away from time to time."

"Do you miss him?"

"Do you?" Philippa went into the attack.

"He's not *my* boy-friend," Cathy shrugged.

"He isn't mine either." Philippa stood up. "I'll make us some tea."

She was busy in the kitchenette when she became aware that Cathy had come to watch her.

"It would be nice if you married him, Philippa. He's too good for you to let someone else take him."

"Why don't *you* take him?"

"Two weeks from now I'll be with Alan," said Cathy, as if she had not heard the question. "That's the real reason I like Robin – because he looks like Alan."

"They're both fair-haired. That's the only resemblance. Robin is much stronger."

"I hate strong men. They always end up trying to boss you."

Philippa carried the tea tray into the living room and changed the subject as she changed the venue. An hour later, the chauffeur returned to collect Cathy who, at the sound of his ring, settled herself motionless in the chair where he had deposited her.

"Will you come and see me on Saturday?" she asked as she was picked up. "Marius won't be home. He and Celia have been invited away for the weekend."

"I don't care if he is home," Philippa lied.

"Then you'll come?"

"Yes." Only as Cathy left did Philippa regret her promise. Even entering Marius's house was becoming more than she could bear. Much as she hated the thought of the impending cruise and all the deceit it involved, it would take her away from England, and when she returned it would be without Cathy.

168

Marius would be furious with her for not telling him what his niece had been planning, and though she shrank from the thought of the ugly scene that lay ahead of her with him, she knew it would at least be the final one. Afterwards he would never wish to see her again. Not that she would wait to see him either: by then he would be married to Celia.

Tears blurred her vision and she blinked them away. Once the cruise was over she would make a clean break with her past. It meant leaving Fleet Street and finding a job away from journalism, but it was the only way she could begin to put Marius out of her mind.

CHAPTER FOURTEEN

Saturday was an unexpectedly bright day. A pale sun shone out of a blue sky, and a soft breeze rippled the grass in Hyde Park as Philippa bowled through it in a taxi. On an impulse she stopped the cab several hundred yards before her destination and walked the rest of the way, enjoying the exercise and deciding that next weekend she would definitely go down to the country. Her pleasure evaporated as she realised that the week after she would be in Australia. How angry Marius would be! Hastily pushing aside the thought, she mounted the steps and rang the bell.

Cathy came into the hall to greet her, a sign that she was alone in the house apart from the servants.

"I'm glad you decided to come for lunch," she smiled. "I ordered something special as a celebration."

"What are we celebrating?"

"I don't know. I just feel happy."

Philippa looked at her curiously. Cathy did look pleased with herself. "Robin's due back today," she said casually, and knew no surprise when she saw Cathy blush.

"That should give *you* something to celebrate, then," the girl retorted with her usual quick wit, and Philippa wisely decided to make no rejoinder. Lunch was excellent, as was the vintage wine that accompanied it, and it was two sleepy girls who returned to the drawing room and relaxed to music, watching somnolently as the bright blue sky grew hazy and the sun was lost in cloud.

A delicious languor pervaded Philippa, and even though she knew it was caused by wine and not true happiness, she firmly refused to analyse it away. Somewhere in the distance a bell rang and voices were heard, but she was too tired to take any notice, and she remained in her armchair, feet stretched towards the glowing fire. What luxury to have a fire as well as central heating. She yawned and stretched, then stiffened as her hands were caught in a warm clasp. Tilting her head, she saw Robin.

"You're back! How did you know I was here?"

"Guesswork."

"When did you get back to England?"

"An hour ago."

"I'm flattered you came in search of us so soon," she teased, and stole a quick glance at Cathy. There was no mistaking the twin flags of red that burned in the girl's cheeks, nor the brightness of the dark eyes as they rested on the man.

Letting go of Philippa's hands, he strode over to Cathy and tilted her chin to look into her face. "Pleased to see me?"

"I'm always pleased to see my friends. Where did you go?"

"On a long, long journey."

"You must have had good weather. You're as red as a beetroot!"

His smile was brief, replaced by a look compounded of sadness and anxiety. "What would you say to a nice surprise?"

"I'd say yes! Is it something you brought me?"

"You could say that." He turned, and as he walked past Philippa she saw that his expression was still strained. He opened the door, beckoned to someone outside and then stepped back to let another, younger man come forward.

"Alan!" Cathy cried.

"Hello, Cathy," he said, and shuffled forward, hands in the pockets of his jacket, face screwed up in a nervous smile.

"For a couple of lovebirds," Robin drawled, "you're not very lovable!"

Only then did Cathy move. Slowly getting to her feet, she bridged the distance between her and Alan. "I can walk," she said unsteadily.

"So I see." For the first time he appeared moved. "I never thought you would again. Your uncle said – "

"I told you not to believe him."

A look of discomfiture crossed Alan's face, but Cathy did not appear to notice it. "I can't believe you've come back," she bubbled. "I was coming out to *you* in two weeks' time. I've got the tickets and everything. Marius doesn't know, of course, but –"

"Robin told me what you were planning to do," Alan interrupted. "That's why he made me come back with him."

"He *made* you. . . ." Cathy faltered and stopped, then spoke again. "What do you mean come back *with* him? I don't understand."

Alan glanced over his shoulder to Robin, silently leaning against the door, his arms across his chest. For someone so easy-going and bland, he looked particularly angry, as though his thoughts were unpleasant. Realising he was being left on his own, Alan turned back to Cathy. "Robin flew out to see me," he explained. "He told me you intended joining me and he – he made me see that if you lied to your uncle like this he'd never forgive you."

"I don't care if he doesn't! I was coming out because I wanted to be with you."

"Wanted or want?" Robin asked, speaking to Cathy for the first time since Alan had come into the room.

She stared at him, and even across a wide distance, their glances seemed to hold and lock. "I don't know what you mean."

"Yes, you do. For heaven's sake be honest with yourself, if not with anyone else. Is it want or *wanted* to be with Alan?"

Cathy turned away from him and moved closer to Alan. The colour came and went in her face as it did in his, but they made no move to touch, and after a long moment she stepped back and sat down in a nearby chair.

"What's happened?" she whispered. "I've been counting the hours till we met, and now you're here. . . . I don't understand. Help me, Alan."

Once again he turned to look at the older man, but Robin still stared back at him implacably, and Alan straightened his shoulders and moved to Cathy's side.

"The only way I can help you is to tell you the truth," he said bluntly. "You won't like it, but it's what I've got to do – what I came back to do." The tip of his tongue came out and ran along the edge of his lips, an apprehensive gesture that indicated fear. "If it hadn't been for Robin I wouldn't be here now. He bought me the ticket and he threatened to – and he made me see it would be much worse for me if I let you come to Australia without telling you the truth."

Cathy lifted her head. "What truth?"

"That your coming would ruin all my plans."

"Plans for what?"

He hesitated, his embarrassment tangible. "For a workshop of my own."

"You had those plans when you were here," Cathy reminded him.

"But no chance of achieving them! That's why I went to Australia. With your uncle's money I stood a chance of getting my own place before I was too old to run it!"

"I don't understand." Cathy looked fierce, as if she did understand but was afraid to admit it to herself. "I know Marius found you a job and bought you your ticket, but – "

"It was more than that." Alan's voice was strangled. "He gave me three thousand pounds, too, and promised me the same amount each year till I'd saved enough to open a place of my own. With his money, plus what I earn myself, I'll be able to do it in three years' time. And it won't be a poky workshop either. It'll be a sensational place. Capable of tuning and repairing any make of car in the world!" He flung out his hands. "That's why I came back with Robin. I had to warn you not to come out to me. If you do, it will ruin everything."

Philippa jumped to her feet, her one thought to be close to Cathy. But as she moved forward, Robin's arm came out and restrained her. Quietly she sat down again, acknowledging that at this moment Cathy had to be left alone to find her own words for her own tragedy.

"What you're trying to tell me," Cathy said in a high-pitched voice, "is that if we're together, my uncle will stop giving you

173

three thousand a year, and you'd rather have his money and a workshop than me."

"I can't support you unless I'm in a proper position."

"I don't think support comes into it." Cathy was not Marius Lyon's niece for nothing, and the contempt in her voice was apparent. "You'd have married me if you could have been sure of having Marius's money too. But now that he's convinced you it has to be one or the other, you've settled for the money."

"I had no choice. He told me you'd never walk again. He said if I took you away with me he'd wash his hands of you."

"We didn't need his help," Cathy said angrily. "We could have managed."

"You talk like that because you don't know what it means to live on a budget. You've always had everything you've wanted and – "

"Couples get married earning far less than you were," she said scornfully.

"Ordinary couples, yes, but not when the wife's an invalid. And that's what Marius said you'd be. How did I know he was lying?"

"You could have asked my doctor."

"I could just see him talking to *me*." Alan was equally angry now. "If I'd gone round to see him he'd have thrown me out on my ear."

"Then you could have asked *me*."

"How could I do that?" he said violently. "Your uncle said you didn't know how ill you were."

"There was still something you could have done," she persisted. "I don't know what, but – " A bleak look settled on her face. "But I'm sure there was something."

Helplessly Alan stared at her. "It wouldn't have worked for us, Cathy, not if you'd been in a wheelchair for life. That's what frightened me more than anything. I could have managed the money side of it – I'll admit that – but what I couldn't face was being tied to an invalid. That's why I accepted your uncle's offer."

"Why didn't you tell me the truth?"

"I didn't want to hurt you."

"Would you have married me if Marius hadn't said he'd wash his hands of me if we eloped again?"

"Of course I would," Alan said quickly. "At least with his help I could have given you all the luxuries you were used to. Had someone to look after you and – "

"Spare me the details," Cathy cut in contemptuously. "My uncle was right after all. It *was* his money you wanted. *I* came second."

"Don't be bitter, Cathy."

"I'm not," she said quietly. "I'm just furious that Marius was right."

Alan shuffled his feet. "Will you say anything to him? I mean there's no reason why you should tell him what you were going to do. You can go off on the cruise proper and he'll be none the wiser."

"I think he'd find it amusing to be told the truth. It will give *him* a chance to say I told you so!"

"He'll be furious with you. Say nothing, Cathy."

"Don't worry about me, Alan. If Marius throws me out I won't come running to you! Anyway, you'll come out of the story looking pure and white. I'll tell Marius you were so anxious not to go back on your agreement with him that you flew over from Australia to stop me. He may even decide to increase your stay-away-from-me allowance!"

"Don't put it like that," he said defensively.

"What other way should I put it? Perhaps you'd rather I told him to stop sending you any money at all? After all, if I've no intention of marrying you, he doesn't need to pay you for keeping away from me!"

Alan turned a sickly yellow, and seeing it, Cathy laughed cruelly. "Don't worry, I wouldn't let him do that. Helping to buy your workshop is a small price to pay for learning the sort of person you are."

"Things could have worked out for us," he said huskily. "If

you hadn't had that accident, we'd have been married by now."

"I'm glad we're not," she replied. "I'm pretty despicable myself, but not so despicable that I deserve you!"

Alan turned on his heel and walked out. Robin glanced at Cathy and then also left the room, careful to close the door behind him.

Philippa did not know what to say or do. There was a look on Cathy's face that prevented her from offering sympathy, and so she remained where she was and waited.

"Why don't I feel as upset as I should?" Cathy asked suddenly. "Do you think it's because I'm so badly hurt that I've gone numb?"

"Perhaps you're not hurt at all. It might just be your pride."

"You don't have much pride when you've spent four months in a wheelchair." She glanced at the door. "All I feel is a sort of relief."

"Then we should be grateful to Alan for coming here. At least he saved you an unnecessary journey."

"Robin saved us the journey," said Cathy, "not Alan. Tell me the truth, Philippa, were you really in the dark about his going to Australia?"

"Absolutely."

"I expect Marius sent him." There was a hard note in Cathy's voice. "He must have been scared I'd try and get to Alan somehow and decided I should be told the truth before I made a complete fool of myself."

"Why not ask Robin?" said Philippa, as she heard the door open behind her. "He's here now."

"I will." Cathy flung out her hand in an imperious gesture to the tall, fair-haired man who stood some distance away from her. "Did Marius send you to bring Alan back?"

"No. Your uncle believes I went to spend a week's holiday in Scotland. My trip to Australia was my own idea."

"But why? You didn't know what arrangements Marius had made with Alan."

"I only knew I didn't believe *your* version of what had happened. I couldn't see your uncle as the sort of man who would stop you from marrying someone if he genuinely believed they loved you. If I'd been on equal terms with Mr. Lyon, I would have asked him to his face to tell me the truth, but even though I was in love with his niece I didn't feel I had the right to question what he'd done. The only way I could find out was to ask the only other person who knew. That was Alan."

"So you went to Australia and saved me from making an idiot of myself," Cathy concluded.

"And also saved you from hurting your uncle. Alan's right about that, Cathy. There's no reason for him to know what you were going to do."

"I intend telling him the truth," she reiterated. "He's going to be very grateful to you, Robin. He might even make you an editor of one of his papers!"

Robin said an extremely rude word, and Cathy looked at him reprovingly. "Don't you want to become an editor?"

"On my own merits." He was unexpectedly angry. "It wasn't a desire to further my career that sent me to Australia."

"I know that," she said coolly. "You've already admitted it's because you love me."

"So," he glared. "What are you going to do about it?"

"I'm waiting to see what *you* will do."

"Nothing," he said. "I've done as much as I intend to."

"Then it's my move," Cathy replied, and got up to go to him. Her foot caught in the rug and she stumbled and clutched at the back of a chair to save herself from falling. "I was all set to fly halfway round the world to a man who didn't exist," she gasped. "Yet now I can't walk halfway across the room to *you!*"

In two strides he was beside her, lifting her up bodily to place her on the settee. "You've a lot of growing up to do," he growled, "but I love you and I'm willing to wait."

"How quickly can I grow?" she whispered, and putting her arms around his neck, pulled his face down to hers.

Philippa tiptoed from the room. She was still amazed at the ease with which Cathy had accepted the truth about Alan, and with bitter irony realised that Marius's assessment of his niece

177

had been better than her own. Perhaps Celia's efforts to keep Cathy a child had made her turn blindly to the first man who had made her feel a woman. But all this was in the past. Cathy's future held Robin; a young man of intelligence and integrity who would help her to find her true potential.

Pleasure for her friends' future made her aware of the bleakness of her own. Marius too would be getting married, and the thought of him and Celia together was so painful that she knew she could not continue working for him. She would give Kennedy her resignation on Monday. But in the meantime she would go back to her flat and stay there.

She was halfway through the front door when Robin's voice stopped her. "Where are you sneaking off to, Philippa?"

She swung round. "I thought you and Cathy would like to be alone."

"Stuff it," he said inelegantly, and opening the door behind him, indicated for her to come back into the drawing room.

With reluctance she did so, though this was swamped by the pleasure she felt at the sight of Cathy's beaming face.

"Do you think Marius will approve of Robin, or will I have to elope with him too?"

"I'm sure he'll approve," Philippa said warmly.

"Then perhaps he'll be able to persuade Robin that we needn't be engaged for a year."

"I won't change my mind about that," Robin interrupted firmly. "I want to make sure I'm not getting you on the rebound."

"You know you're not," she protested. "If I hadn't been furious with Marius I wouldn't have been so obstinate about Alan."

"We're still not rushing into marriage. I want you to go on your cruise – a real cruise, too, no sneaking off this time and going somewhere else."

"Beast!" Cathy protested.

"And when you come back," he went on, "I'll start courting you in the real old-fashioned way."

Cathy giggled. "Celia's going to be furious. She'll never get

Marius to disapprove of *you*, and once I'm married, her days here will be numbered. She'll have to accept his offer and find a place of her own."

"Not now," Philippa said mechanically, and stopped as she felt two pairs of eyes looking at her with curiosity. Too late she remembered her promise to Marius not to say anything about his marriage. Yet it seemed pointless to maintain secrecy over something that would no longer worry Cathy. "Your uncle's going to marry Celia," she told her.

"Don't be silly," Cathy said positively. "At one time I was afraid he would, but not any more. You shouldn't believe a word Celia tells you. It's all wishful thinking."

"It wasn't only Celia who told me. Marius did so too."

This did startle Cathy. "*Marius* told you? When?"

"The night of the staff party."

"Why hasn't he told me?"

"He knows you don't like Celia. That's why he's kept it quiet. I think their intention is to – to get married when you're on the cruise."

"Do *you* think so?" Cathy asked Robin.

"Could be," he said non-committally.

"It's true," Philippa reiterated, and afraid she would burst into tears regardless of who was watching her, she turned blindly to the door. "I'll go home if you don't mind," she said indistinctly, and not waiting for a reply, ran into the hall.

She was at the front door again when Robin came after her.

"I'll see you home," he said, "and I'd also like to apologise. Cathy and I have been so involved with each other that we've overlooked the way you must be feeling."

"I feel fine," she lied. "I'm delighted for you both."

"I was referring to you and Marius," he said, guiding her down the steps. "I was hoping you'd got over him, but you obviously haven't."

"I will." A taxi went past and she signalled it to stop. "Don't bother seeing me home, Robin. I'd rather go alone."

"I'll come with you for the ride."

"No." Quickly she clambered in and closed the door. "Please

go back to Cathy. I'd rather be by myself."

"If that's what you wish." He stepped back, but remained on the pavement until the taxi turned the corner and was no longer in sight.

Philippa was oppressed by the solitude of her flat, and she walked restlessly from the bedroom to the sitting room to the kitchen. It was impossible to close her mind to everything that had happened today, and memory of the happiness that lay ahead for Cathy and Robin increased her own self-pity.

Annoyed with herself, she decided to do some work. Luckily she had brought home a folder of letters, and she began to go through them, but even immersing herself in other people's problems did not help her to forget her own, and she pushed the pile of letters away from her and rested her head in her hands.

Thank goodness she had made Marius believe she was engaged to Robin. At least because of this he would never know the real truth behind her resignation from the paper. He would see it as her unwillingness to go on working in proximity with Robin, rather than her passionate desire to get away from *him*. Angry that Marius was again uppermost in her mind, she went into the kitchen to make a cup of tea, pausing in the hall as she caught sight of herself in the mirror. How pale and thin she was! No wonder Robin was sorry for her. She touched the smudge of violet below her eyes and turned away from the deep sadness in them.

A bell rang sharply and she stopped, startled. It rang again and her surprise turned to apprehension.

"Who is it?" she asked, stepping forward but not opening the door.

"Marius."

Her heart began to pound. What was he doing in London and why was he outside her flat?

"Open the door," he ordered.

Her fingers fumbled at the lock and he pushed the door wide

and stepped in, dwarfing the tiny hall with his height and bulk.

"I th-thought you were away for the – the weekend," she stammered.

"I couldn't face another day of it. I had to see you."

"Me?" Her mouth was dry and she had such difficulty speaking that she decided it would be safer not to try.

"Yes, you," he said harshly. "But half the things I planned to say don't seem to be necessary any more." He grabbed her arm and pulled her roughly into the living room. "What game are you playing at?" he burst out. "Why did you make me believe you were engaged to Robin when all the time – " He gave her a shake that set her teeth rattling. "Why did you want me to believe he was going to marry you?"

She could think of no reasonable lie that would satisfy him, for he was glaring at her with such fury that she felt nothing she said would meet with his approval.

"Well," he shouted, "I'm waiting for your answer."

"I don't have to answer. You're not my keeper "

"I'm going to be!" He was still shouting and, aware of it, he suddenly lowered his voice. "Philippa," he said unsteadily, "didn't you hear what I said?"

"Yes," she said brightly, and taking advantage of his loosened grip, put the distance of the room between them. Yet what a small distance it was; one that he could easily bridge in three steps. Two, being Marius.

"I'm sure you're pleased about Cathy and Robin," she went on brightly, "and I suppose you'd like to – to show your appreciation to me, but – but it isn't necessary. I just played a long shot and it came off."

"My desire to keep you has nothing to do with appreciation for bringing Robin into Cathy's life. I want you, Philippa, and 'm pretty sure you want me."

"I don't want you," she said, remembering he was going to marry Celia.

"You do! Cathy said – "

"Cathy?" Philippa cried, and all at once knew what had

happened. Robin had told Cathy she was in love with Marius and Cathy had misguidedly told Marius himself. "You surely don't believe anything Cathy tells you? She's the world's worst liar. Just because I flirted with you it doesn't mean I want you. You're very attractive, Marius, and very important. That's enough to turn any girl's head."

His skin went even more ruddy. It made his hair look startling grey and showed her again how white it had become around the temples. "Why should Cathy lie to me?" he asked.

"She'd say anything to stop you from marrying Celia, surely you know that."

"Ah yes, Celia." Marius took a step forward. He was much closer to Philippa now. "I was forgetting Celia."

"I thought you were." She forced a laugh. "You like women too much, Marius, but even in this permissive age men don't usually have a fiancée and a mistress!"

"I don't have either," he said heavily, "and for the past four months I haven't had a woman at all."

"It can't have been from lack of opportunity." Philippa was speaking without knowing what she was saying.

"It was lack of desire. If I couldn't have the woman I wanted then I didn't want anyone at all."

Still he remained where he was, yet the magnetism that exuded from him began to envelop her, and a tremor ran through her body, so that she started to shake.

"I'm surprised Celia's playing so hard to get," she said in her brightest voice.

"For pity's sake!" he cried. "Don't you know what I'm trying to say?"

Philippa refused to believe what her senses were telling her. She wanted Marius so desperately that she was afraid her need for him was making her see more in his words than was there. From somewhere within her she found an unexpected source of strength and it gave her the courage to tilt her head and look at him squarely.

"Pity's the one thing I don't need, Marius. If you want to show me how pleased you are that I introduced Robin to Cathy then make sure Kennedy gives me a good reference."

Marius looked at her blankly. "A reference?"

"When I leave. I've wanted to get a job abroad for a long time, but you played on my guilt and made it impossible for me to go. Now Cathy's got Robin, I'm free."

"You're not free. You're mine." His hand came out and sent the chair between them crashing to the floor. "Mine!" he repeated, and pulled her so hard against him that the breath was crushed from her body. "I'm never going to let you go. If Cathy's wrong and you don't love me, then I'll have to make you change your mind, even if it takes me the rest of my life."

"How can you talk to me like this?" she cried. "You're going to marry Celia. You told me so."

"You told me you were going to marry Robin, and you were lying. Do you think it's only women who have pride?"

"You mean – "

"I mean I love *you*! Only you. That night at the party when you said you were engaged, I could have killed you. Then when you asked about Celia I let you believe what you wanted." His hands cupped her face. "From the moment I met you, there's been no one else. It's very wearing on my nerves," he said in a cracked voice. "I don't enjoy being a celibate."

"Poor Marius," she cried, trembling between laughter and tears.

"Poor indeed, without you," he whispered, and rested his cheek on hers. Aware that she was still not relaxed, he moved his head and looked into her eyes. "What's on your mind still?"

"Celia. *She* told me she was going to marry you; she actually said so."

"Knowing you, my darling, you probably put the words into her mouth."

Philippa tried to think back, but she was too aware of the arms that were holding her to be capable of cohesive thought. Besides, what did the past matter when the future was so wonderful? She trembled violently, and Marius caught her up into his arms and carried her across to the settee. Holding her tightly, he sat down with her and she nestled against him.

"I still can't believe it," she murmured. "When did you know you loved me?"

"When you walked into my office and confessed you were the person who had told Cathy to elope."

"But you fired me!"

"In order not to see you again." He looked unexpectedly fierce. "I'm too old for you, Philippa; you need a young man."

"I need you." She twined her fingers through his thick hair. "Anyway, you once said it was the age of the mother that mattered!" She heard him catch his breath and knew he was as responsive to her nearness as she was to his.

"You can seduce me with words like that," he said jerkily, and he was no longer the public image he presented to the world, but a man tormented by his desire for one woman. "If only I were ten years younger," he groaned.

"Or I were ten years older. I'm too young for you, Marius. You'll think me childish and inexperienced."

"It's so long since I kissed you, I can't remember if you are!"

His mouth fastened on hers, and knowing herself loved and not just desired, there was nothing to prevent her from responding. Unashamedly she let him see how much she needed him, pressing herself close to him and undoing the buttons of his shirt to touch his skin. The hair on his chest was rough against her fingers and she pulled at it, feeling him shudder with emotion as she did so. Then his hands were warm on her body, caressing her roundness and cupping the curve of her breasts. Her hands moved along his back and with a groan he pushed her violently away from him. His face was pale and there was a film of perspiration along the top of his lip. It gave him a look of utter vulnerability, and knowing she had put it there, she could have wept for him.

"I'm yours, Marius!" she cried.

"Not till I've put a wedding ring on your finger, which will be in three days' time, young woman," he said shakily. "I'm not having you say I seduced you into marrying me."

"Would you mind very much if *you* had to say it instead?"

"I wouldn't mind at all."

"Well then," she murmured, and put her arms around him.

4 FREE
Harlequin Romances

TAKE THESE 4 Harlequin Romances FREE

Delight in **Mary Wibberley**'s warm romance MAN OF POWER, the story of a girl whose life changes from drudgery to glamour overnight....Let THE WINDS OF WINTER by **Sandra Field** take you on a journey of love to Canada's beautiful Maritimes....Thrill to a cruise in the tropics— and a devastating love affair in the aftermath of a shipwreck—in **Rebecca Stratton**'s THE LEO MAN....Travel to the wilds of Kenya in a quest for love with the determined heroine in **Karen van der Zee**'s exciting LOVE BEYOND REASON.

Harlequin Romances . . . 6 exciting novels published each month! Each month you will get to know interesting, appealing, true-to-life people . . . . You'll be swept to distant lands you've dreamed of visiting . . . . Intrigue, adventure, romance, and the destiny of many lives will thrill you through each Harlequin Romance novel.

Get all the latest books before they're sold out!

As a Harlequin subscriber you actually receive your personal copies of the latest Romances immediately after they come off the press, so you're sure of getting all 6 each month.

Cancel your subscription whenever you wish!

You don't have to buy any minimum number of books. Whenever you decide to stop your subscription just let us know and we'll cancel all further shipments.

Your FREE gift includes

- MAN OF POWER by **Mary Wibberley**
- THE WINDS OF WINTER by **Sandra Field**
- THE LEO MAN by **Rebecca Stratton**
- LOVE BEYOND REASON by **Karen van der Zee**

FREE GIFT CERTIFICATE

and Subscription Reservation

Mail this coupon today!

Harlequin Reader Service

In the U.S.A.
1440 South Priest Drive
Tempe, AZ 85281

In Canada
649 Ontario Street
Stratford, Ontario N5A 6W2

Please send me my 4 Harlequin Romance novels FREE.
Also, reserve a subscription to the 6 NEW Harlequin
Romance novels published each month. Each month I will
receive 6 NEW Romance novels at the low price of $1.50
each (*Total–$9.00 a month*). There are no shipping and
handling or any other hidden charges. I may cancel this
arrangement at any time, but even if I do, these first 4 books
are still mine to keep.   116 BPR EAKK

NAME	(PLEASE PRINT)

ADDRESS	APT. NO.

CITY

STATE/PROV.	ZIP/POSTAL CODE

Offer not valid to present subscribers

Offer expires March 31, 1984

If price changes are necessary you will be notified.